BIRD SUIT

SYDNEY HEGELE

Invisible Publishing
Fredericton | Halifax | Picton

Library and Archives Canada Cataloguing in Publication
Title: Bird suit / Sydney Hegele.
Names: Hegele, Sydney, author.
Description: First edition.
Identifiers: Canadiana (print) 20230502709
          Canadiana (ebook) 20230502717
          ISBN 9781778430428 (softcover)
          ISBN 9781778430435 (EPUB)
Subjects: LCGFT: Novels.
Classification: LCC PS8615.E324 B57 2024 | DDC C813/.6—dc23

Edited by Annick MacAskill
Cover and interior design by Megan Fildes with thanks to Haiti Tynes
Typeset in Laurentian | With thanks to type designer Rod McDonald

Invisible Publishing is committed to protecting our natural environment. As part of our efforts, both the cover and interior of this book are printed on acid-free 100% post-consumer recycled fibres.

Printed and bound in Canada.

Invisible Publishing | Fredericton, Halifax, & Picton
www.invisiblepublishing.com

Published with the generous assistance of the Canada Council for the Arts, the Ontario Arts Council, and the Government of Canada.

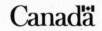

For Christian, Camille, Mom,
and for my own Birds.

Deo gratias.

I think the sirens in *The Odyssey*
sang *The Odyssey,* for there is nothing more seductive, more terrible,
than the story of our own life, the
one we do not want to hear and
will do anything to listen to.

—Mary Ruefle

There is a bird and a stone
in your body. Your job is not
to kill the bird with the stone.

—Victoria Chang

THE FIRST PART OF BIRD SUIT

CALLED

BLOOM

THE PORT PETER PEACHES LURE TOURISTS, city folk from the southern side of Lake Ligeia. The Red Haven semi-freestones are fist big and full of nectar, with lightly fuzzed skin over firm, yellow flesh. Every season, tourists learn the Red Havens will not give up their pits until fully ripe.

Supermarkets and convenience stores set up fold-out tables on the sidewalks outside their shops. The peaches are six dollars a basket, then five, then four. Food trucks sell funnel cake covered in peaches and ice cream—extra peaches are free. There are too many, and they will only be perfect to eat for a couple of weeks or so. The tourists eat the peaches until they puke on the ten-cents-a-ride carousel in the middle of town. They chase the peaches with cheap lager at the Hanged Man pub. They stumble along the boardwalk at night until they reach the beach, and they wade around in Lake Ligeia's dark green water, trying to wash off the sticky sweetness.

What makes a Port Peter peach so perfect? The conditions in which they are grown are not any different from those in the other small towns that surround Lake Ligeia. Peaches prefer freezing winters and sweltering summers. Several cool summers in a row wreck years of grapes in Ivey and plums in Hewitt. But the Port Peter peaches never shrink. They never ripen too early or too late.

The boardwalk is lined with ice cream stands and custom T-shirt shops and knock-off fortune tellers and real fortune tellers. Every shop is open until three in the morning. The tourists buy lighthouse shot glasses and floppy hats that say *Practise What You Peach* and paper bags of crispy French fries soaked in oil. Every room in the Super 8 hotel is booked.

The tourists ignore burnt butts on the boardwalk and coffee cups half-buried in the sand and the metal sign that used to read *NOT SAFE FOR SWIMMING*, but now just reads *NO SAFE*. They gorge on sweet peaches while the town is hot and humming with life.

Most of the tourists are boy-men who wear *I LOVE CANADA* T-shirts that go down to their knees with basketball shorts, even though they don't play basketball. On the poorly lit boardwalk at night, the boy-men could be sixteen or thirty-six years old—it's hard to tell. They spend their nights splitting birthday cake vodka with local girls, making promises they can't keep. I'll bring you back with me, they say.

September sneaks up on the tourists. They never expect it, even though it arrives every year. The peaches are suddenly too soft. The juice is tinged sour. When their fingers can squish through the bruised flesh of the fruit without much effort, they know it is time to return home.

In September, the boardwalk shops close when the sun sets. The food trucks close and drive back to the city. It is too cold for ice cream. Too cold to swim. The tourists leave as quickly as they arrive, and suddenly, the town's population drops to one thousand people.

The real Port Peter is a tourism town in hibernation. The souvenir shops and restaurants and bars and boutiques lay off most of their staff. Seasonal contracts end. Townies in thin windbreakers buy coffees with dimes and stand in line outside the unemployment office. They arrive and leave empty-handed, day after day; there are no new jobs to give out, but they continue to show up anyway. To get up early and have a hot drink with their neighbours is their job, in a way, and they think of it with an odd kind of fondness.

Winter in Port Peter is wet cold. Morning rain soaks the pines, and by nightfall the branches are covered in ice, sharp spikes ready to snap and fall. Lake Ligeia freezes over, and fearless kids walk out onto the ice and play soccer baseball. Leftover snowballs harden into dirt-laden chunks on roadsides, hard enough to hurt if thrown. And they are thrown. And they do hurt.

When the housing market crashes in '08, the people of Port Peter use their squirrel funds of summer money to pay for mortgages and rent and groceries and gas. They have nothing left to spend on tourist beer and tourist food and tourist artisan goods that would help local businesses. Summer and winter become a dramatic boom and bust. Residents make most of their meals out of the Red Haven peaches that they canned in the summer: peach butter and peach crisp and peach pie and peach salad and peach cobbler and peach jam on bright white packaged bread that never moulds. The Port Peter food bank runs out of an abandoned building on Elizabeth Street that used to be Barbershop and Billiards. Dust-covered hairdresser chairs and broken pool cues and damp cardboard boxes filled with office supplies litter the floor like in an FBI raid. Loose wires hang from the ceiling. Half the fluorescent lights stopped working years back, but the other half flicker rapidly. Cans of sweet peaches stacked high.

Most people in Port Peter have had gout at some point in their lives. The purines in the peaches increase their blood's uric acid levels. When they have flare-ups, the urgent care doctor in town puts them back on prednisone—a corticosteroid to help the inflammation. The prednisone makes their faces bloat like hamsters with cheeks full of seed.

Nine months after tourist season, the Port Peter girls give birth in bar bathrooms and school smoking pits and on ripped floral couches in their fathers' apartments.

Every girl in Port Peter knows what follows. Port Peter only has one urgent care clinic, run out of a Roman Catholic Church parish hall. Patients are made to hold baby shoes and hear heartbeats. They can go to the city for an abortion, but there is only one Greyhound bus that goes through Port Peter each day, and it leaves at noon when most of the girls are at work.

The girls go to the cliffside lookout off County Road Five, where there is a white plastic laundry basket with a pink fitted sheet inside. This is where the Port Peter girls leave their babies for the Birds.

The women of the town tell one another about the Birds in secret, like sending carrier pigeons across enemy lines. When a Port Peter girl gets pregnant by a tourist boy, a woman in her life gives her all the information she needs to know. Older sisters. Cousins. Female teachers. Babysitters. Great-aunts. This ensures that children are not stuck raising children.

People cannot say with any certainty that the creatures are more bird than girl or more girl than bird. The local folklore has evolved over the decades. The oldest stories talk of feathered sirens emerging from Lake Ligeia in white lace dresses, dripping water and tangled in their own dark hair. Every generation adds new details. Black teeth. Silver lockets with the eyes of men inside. Scales. Gills. Fur. Hooves. Eventually, the creatures are just called Birds. Ruthless, beautiful Birds—hungry for the blood of sacrifice.

The mothers of the girls pack their daughters into pickups and drive them to the cliffside lookout. They sit in their trucks with their hazards on while the girls walk to the lookout in flip-flops and May sundresses.

The girls stop when they find the white plastic laundry basket with a pink fitted sheet. They kiss the babies' sweaty foreheads and leave them squirming in the dark. When the girls go back the next morning, the basket is almost always empty.

1986 - 2007

Georgia Jackson grows up around dead things. She is six years old the first time she watches her mother work at Buck Deco, a taxidermy shop where Elsie started as a cashier shortly after Georgia was born. When a new animal arrives, Elsie measures, fleshes, salts, and builds moulds out of polyurethane foam before she sews skin shut and paints glass eyes. She screws moose antlers into wooden mounts and combs out matted fox fur. At home, Georgia cuts her own stuffed animals open with craft scissors and empties them of their cotton fluff, just so she can restuff them and staple them closed again, bringing them back to life.

Glass display cases sit upright against Buck Deco's baby-blue walls, beneath wood beams with live bark edges. Every available space in the shop is taken up by an animal: blue butterflies with paper-thin wings pinned to black boards, Arctic fox pups dressed in tweed jackets and reading glasses, stuffed garter snakes hanging from the ceiling like shoe-laces. Each time something new comes in, Elsie Jackson must remove an older display to make room, though she will never throw an animal away. She hides what she can in the back room and takes the rest home. Georgia and Elsie have had many family pets—just not live ones.

Throughout her childhood, Georgia finds comfort in the cyclical nature of death. Each peach in Port Peter begins as a seed that grows, ripens, falls to the ground, rots, and returns to its roots. An inevitability. A predictability. No matter what Georgia does—where she lives, who she loves—there is nothing she can do to prevent her eventual departure from the world. It is okay that her father left before she was born because, eventually, everything leaves, and everything returns.

Georgia's interests diversify as she grows. She covers the walls of her bedroom with pages ripped out of her favourite books. *Matilda. It. Othello.* Pages yellowed and curled at the edges. Hot-pink curtains and white shelves full of porcelain dolls and a small TV with a VCR that only works if Georgia places a round rock under the tape she is trying to play. Her stacks of stolen library books are on the floor by her bed, spines cracked and covers ripped and margins full of handwriting. The stuffed animals with surgery scars sit in the back of her closet.

In eighth grade, Georgia is cast as an ensemble member in an original play written by her school's music teacher. The story is based on a dream Mr. Marshall had during an edible-induced twenty-seven-hour sleep. The students only ever call him the Roach because his tweed jackets reek like weed and the two ends of his skinny moustache look like the antennae of a bug. The Roach is an established pianist: a term he uses to describe himself because he almost got into Juilliard, which practically makes him an alumnus. The play has no dialogue—only an hour-long series of tableaux that are meant to represent every individual battle in the War of 1812, accompanied by an original piano score that the Roach plays himself, on a keyboard, on stage, during the play. Georgia and the other cast members wear redcoat jackets and ballet leotards with no pants. The Roach makes each student drink a shot of espresso before they get on stage, and then he shouts things like FEEL the music in your bones, in your very being, in your blood vessels, let it flow through you like DNA! And Georgia says, DNA doesn't even work like that, and the Roach says, Speak for yourself.

There is a synchronicity between body and sound that takes place. The way the Roach's music has a physicality, pulling her from place to place. She doesn't have to worry about knowing what to do—the notes know for her. It is terrifying and incredible. It is a high. She becomes addicted to the vibrancy of performance. In Buck Deco, helping her mother with taxidermy, Georgia is reminded of her own eventual death; on stage, she remembers that she is alive.

When Georgia is twenty, she decides that she will audition for acting school in the city. Her mother supports this. Georgia writes an original monologue, and Elsie helps her practise it after their shifts at Buck Deco have ended for the day.

On the night before Elsie is supposed to drive her daughter to the city for the audition, Georgia begins to panic.

<u>Reasons That Georgia Emily Jackson Is a Terrible,</u>
<u>Despicable Person with No Hope of Redemption</u>

By Georgia Emily Jackson

- 1986. She drives her birth father away while she is still in the womb.

- 1986. Her mother leaves her in a basket on the cliffside to die shortly after she is born. Elsie changes her mind, of course, and retrieves Georgia before her tiny fingers and toes turn blue and fall off, but the original act cannot be undone. Georgia feels it in her lower belly sometimes—a heaviness that is part of the fabric of who she is. Her mother has never owned up to her intention. She tells Georgia from a young age that she left her on the cliffside to be adopted by sirens.

The Birds make better mothers than teenagers do, Elsie says. I thought I was giving you a better life.

Then where are all the other babies?

They live in giant sunken ships beneath Lake Ligeia. They are one big family.

But Georgia Jackson has never been the gullible type, and it doesn't take her long to decide with certainty that anyone in Port Peter who talks about the Birds is a liar. They are ashamed of throwing their children into the lake or leaving them to freeze to death, and they would rather make up a fantastical explanation than own up to their actions.

Why would I lie about that? her mother says. Listen out your bedroom window at night, in the summertime. Hold your breath so that you are as quiet as you can be. You'll hear the Birds singing.

Georgia has tried. She has never heard a thing. Not once.

• 1987. She and Elsie live with the Bloom twins, Arlo and Roselyn—friends of Elsie's. When Georgia only three months old, Arlo leaves, and Roselyn leaves with him, and Elsie scrambles to find a place for Georgia and her to live. Georgia doesn't remember much from this time in her life, but she assumes that she was badly behaved enough to have scared both Blooms out of town.

- 1997. The case of Mark I. He is Elsie Jackson's first long-term relationship since her high school boyfriend. Greasy curls pulled back in a bun. Big arms. Short legs. Construction worker. Drives a red truck from the fifties with no seatbelts. Calls Elsie Honey Bunches of Oats. Georgia is five when he arrives. She is ten when he leaves. Georgia pretends that she and Elsie are Russian spies hiding in witness protection. She learns a few sentences in Russian to make the performance convincing—keeps an accent going for a whole month. Mark I calls Georgia a filthy bitch when he finds out. He tells Elsie that her daughter is a curse. He takes all the furniture with him on his way out of town. Elsie and Georgia sleep together on the pullout couch until Joshua-Jonathan's arrival a year later.

- 1998. The case of Joshua-Jonathan. The Mark I rebound. Bald. Six foot seven. Toothpick thin. Smells like watermelon gum and Axe body spray. Children's contemporary dance instructor at PAPA (Port Academy for the Performing Arts). Drinks tonic water for the taste. Will kick you hard in the shin if you call him JJ. Rides a yellow bike that he says he bought but definitely stole. Calls Elsie wifey after two dates. Moves in after three. He buys the Jacksons new beds, a new couch, a new dishwasher, and a Dalmatian puppy named Cher (his choice, not theirs). He screams at Cher when he's angry. He is always angry. One evening, eleven-year-old Georgia walks Cher up to the top of the escarpment and sets her free in the woods with a bag of Goldfish crackers tied to her collar. She does this so that Cher will be safe. Joshua-Jonathan knocks three of Georgia's teeth out. He tells Georgia that the core of her is rotten, like overripe fruit. Elsie stuffs his clothes in garbage bags and throws them on the front lawn that night, but blames Georgia for the incident. You had to steal the dog? Elsie asks her. Do you know how lonely I am? How lonely it is to be your mother?

- 2003. The case of Mark II. Ginger. Big glasses with lime-green frames. Oversized golf shirts, untucked. Dry skin. Smells like baby powder. Drives a new black hybrid, paid for up front. Art dealer. Calls Elsie baby girl. Calls Georgia baby girl. Never moves out of his townhouse on Queen Street but sleeps over every night. The Jackson house becomes a strange, rundown gallery, filled with real Monets and Pollocks and a Renoir in the dining room that Georgia is not allowed to look at, let alone touch. It should only be looked at by people who appreciate it, Mark II says. Like a beautiful body. You understand, right, baby girl? He looks at Georgia so long that she feels as though he can see right through her clothes and skin, right down to her bones.

Elsie often works late at her taxidermy shop, and Mark II implements mandatory bonding time between him and Georgia while this occurs. He puts on French films without the subtitles. The films always begin with tours of beautiful houses and quickly turn into an hour and a half of violent sex. The women are spat on and beaten and fucked in anger. Mark II masturbates while Georgia keeps her eyes on a bowl of popcorn, too afraid to leave.

I know you're enjoying this, he says. I see the way you look at me when we're alone. You do this to me. You seduce me and I can't control myself.

There is no need for her reciprocation. To Mark II, Georgia's very existence is a siren song. Her long hair, her wide hips, her smile, her silence. And when a man hears a song of his own making, and follows it off the edge of a cliff, falling to his death, it is never his fault. The siren will always be to blame.

Mark II dumps Elsie over the phone later that year, citing Georgia as the reason. *She comes on to me constantly,* he says. *I think it's the not-having-a-dad thing. Makes her want one in all the wrong ways.* He brings the police with him to collect his paintings.

Whenever Georgia and Elsie get into a screaming match, Mark II is brought up. *Sabotage* is the word most often used. *Why couldn't you have been good, just this once? Why can't you be good?*

• 2007. This moment. Georgia is twenty. Georgia is selfishly considering leaving her mother so that she can pursue a dream that will likely amount to nothing. Georgia and Elsie are only sixteen years apart. Georgia cannot imagine a version of her daily life that doesn't include sharing space with Elsie. She cannot imagine leaving her mother alone, ready and available for more disgusting men to move in and hollow her out again.

Elsie is still awake when Georgia gives up trying to sleep. The kitchen reeks like borax. Elsie sits cross-legged on top of the kitchen counter, painting the glass eyes of a large taxidermy crow. A blond pixie cut, cowlicks in all directions. Olive-green overalls, stained with paint and blood and bleach. Earrings made from fox incisors. Toenails painted blue. Her slender fingers are dry and cracked—nails bitten down to the stubs.

I worry about you a lot, Georgia says.

There's nothing for you to worry about, Elsie says. That's a mom job. I'm supposed to do the worrying.

You would call someone if you got hurt and you were here by yourself, right? Georgia asks. You would call someone?

Of course. I would call you.

Right.

You're my best friend, Elsie says. I don't have many friends.

Elsie strokes her daughter's cheek with her thumb.

I like that you'll be making other friends in the city, though, she says. It's kind of like *I'm* making new friends. Like you're just a young me, walking around, doing things I never got to do, and I get to see it from your perspective. Like a video game.

What if I want to stay? Georgia blurts out suddenly. What if I want to live in our house till I'm a hundred years old? And eat off the same plates until I die and then my grand-children will eat off them? And file my taxes with Mike on York Street until taxes don't even exist anymore? What if I want to be Georgia from 33 John Street in the records at the library for all of history? And make sourdough bread with the same starter that you use and give everyone in the neighbourhood loaves that make us feel nostalgic and safe when we eat them?

Elsie looks at her closely. She knows when her daughter is lying.

Georgia thinks for a moment that her mother might tell her she's being ridiculous. Just go to the audition and see what happens, she'll say. Don't stay because of me.

I would love to have you here, Elsie says.

AUGUST 2008

Georgia meanders down Fairground Avenue in her bare feet and eats leftover ice from a blue raspberry slushie with her fingers. It is 2:25 a.m., and navy clouds block out the sliver of a crescent moon.

Sidewalk becomes boardwalk. Lake water splashes up through the spaces between the wooden boards. She cannot see the water, but she feels it between her toes.

Georgia has only swum in Lake Ligeia a handful of times. School teachers used to prohibit swimming on trips to the beach, citing different reasons each year. The undertow. E. coli bacteria. The tourists swim in the lake no matter how rough the conditions, but most locals have been discouraged from water activities for their entire lives. Georgia has a hunch that it is because of Port Peter's namesake: a privateer ship captain named Peter Isobar.

In the late seventeenth century, white American settlers— former Puritans who had renounced their faith and fled New England—slaughtered their way through the already populated lakeside land and claimed it as their own. They could not justify their genocide of the area's Indigenous Peoples by divine providence because they no longer believed in the Winthrop God of cities on hills. They instead told themselves that as victims of rigid Puritan ideology and hard living conditions back in New England, they were forever victims, and were simply committing atrocities in the name of survival. They named their blood-money town New Michigan because of its proximity to a lake, despite Lake Michigan and Lake Ligeia bearing little resemblance to one another.

Captain Peter Isobar crashed his ship, the Grande Arabella, against the rocky cliffs of New Michigan in 1809. It is said that on a completely clear and calm summer night, the entire crew of the Grande Arabella jumped overboard into Lake Ligeia, lured by women singing from the water. Captain Peter was left to man the boat himself, and died on impact. When townspeople searched the wreck the next morning, they found bricks of gold stolen from other ships during the captain's privateering. Three settler families split the loot among themselves. New Michigan was renamed Port Peter and given a new town slogan—A Port of Riches— despite not being a real shipping port. A full-sized model of the Grande Arabella was constructed and anchored in a shallow part of Lake Ligeia in the 1970s. At first it served as a hotel, but it was later converted into an expensive restaurant and jazz bar.

Port Peter has two convenience stores. Little Fish Food Mart is open twenty-four hours. It has American things like Twinkies and Moon Pies and Winston cigarettes. Glass bongs on a shelf behind the front counter. When people steal things, the store manager prints a freeze-frame off the security camera and tapes the photo to the front window under a handmade sign that reads *WALL OF SHAME*. This is where Georgia gets her blue raspberry slushies. The other convenience store is Kyle's Variety on the strip. It has snack-sized bags of all-dressed chips for five dollars more than the grocery store. A freezer at the back full of bags of milk and cans of white grape juice concentrate and jumbo baseball-style hotdogs. The floor is uneven, and people often trip on the ridges between the tiles. No one in Port Peter has ever seen Kyle.

Georgia often spends her nights travelling from one convenience store to the other, watching the tourists as she walks. She scans the crowds on the boardwalk and the downtown strip and the beach, looking for a particular kind of boy-man. Big hands. Agitated sighs. Can't stand still—too anxious to get his dick in a hole or his fist through a wall. These kinds of boy-men leave girls with bruised necks.

The boy-men begin their nights not knowing if they will see the sunrise as lovers or killers because they don't know the difference between their cravings. They grow up with fathers who don't know the difference either—fathers who cheat on their wives and beat their kids and drink to forget their own fathers, who cheated on their wives and beat their kids and drank to forget their own fathers, who cheated on their wives and beat their kids and drank to forget. The boy-men learn that touch can only be violent. They lack both care and power, and that lack feels like a hot stomach ache, low in the belly. And the only medicine is to hurt someone, someone who thinks she deserves it.

Some people seek sex that will transform them—a fuck that makes music sound better and colours seem more saturated—as proof that they are good.

Georgia doesn't try to prove something that she knows is not true. She is not good. Everything that has ever happened to her has been her own fault. If pain doesn't make sense, nothing does. Georgia seeks out tourists who will reinforce this belief. The ones who will wrap their peach-sticky hands around her throat and bring her to the precipice of death. The ones who will say, You deserve this.

The plastic slushie cup is empty when Georgia reaches Kyle's Variety. A bell dings when she opens the door. The store has short aisle shelves and blue fluorescent lights that make Georgia feel like she's walking on the ocean floor. Some of the shelves house things that aren't related to each other: flavoured condoms and orange juice and polymer grow-your-own-girlfriend pills that are meant to be dropped in a glass of water. Georgia used to buy these in middle school. The girlfriend pills grow to ten times their original size. When they are all grown up, they are busty and slimy like salamanders. After a day, they start to mould.

Ryan Frankel is the Kyle's Variety cashier. Georgia went to Peter Isobar Public School and Lakeview High School with him. They played little league soccer, sponsored by the town's AAA hockey team, the Port Peter Pirates. Every time Georgia buys cigarettes, Ryan tries to convince her to join him at Fort Michigan on the outskirts of town on Labour Day and volunteer as a War of 1812 re-enactor. Ryan teaches twelve-year-old boys and retired parks and rec workers how to load a musket in less than ten minutes. He tells Georgia that she can keep at least half of the butter she churns. He is a local, and no local would dare hurt the taxidermist's daughter, even if she asked them to.

Ryan's elbows are propped up on the front counter, blocking the view of the scratch tickets. He's watching a pirated version of *The Dark Knight* on his iPod, squinting to see the screen. Heath Ledger holds up a knife. You wanna know how I got these scars?

I couldn't watch the whole thing, knowing he's dead, Georgia says. Too weird.

Ryan jumps, not expecting Georgia to be less than a foot away. He fumbles with his headphones.

A, um, lady of your stature should not be wandering corner stores at this time of night, he says.

Sure, whatever, Georgia says. Benson & Hedges. King size.

Your mom told me to stop selling you cigarettes.

Good thing she doesn't make the tobacco laws.

Ryan pulls up a plastic flap on the wall behind him and brings out a pack of Benson & Hedges.

Georgia takes a handful of change out of her pocket and drops it on the counter. She sorts the toonies first. Then the loonies. Ryan points to one loonie that shines under the fluorescent light.

This one's a fake, he says. Can't take it.

Bullshit, Georgia snaps. What are you, the guy who makes them?

I can just tell.

Right. Because they had loonies in eighteen-motherfuck-ing-whatever.

I'll buy it, a man's voice says from behind Georgia.

Georgia turns and finds a priest in line behind her, a white clerical collar snug around the base of his throat. Black dress shirt. A smatter of freckles decorating his nose and cheeks, and white-blond curls, greying at the root. He looks to be in his late forties or early fifties.

He looks like someone, Georgia thinks. A reporter on CBC or a contestant on *American Idol* who didn't make it to the Hollywood round. Maybe? Maybe not. She scrunches her face.

You... want to buy my cigarettes?

Yes, the man says. In exchange for the counterfeit loonie.

Georgia snorts.

I collect coins, he continues.

The man reaches down into the leather satchel strapped across him and pulls out a small black binder. He motions Georgia forward with his hand. Rows of plastic pockets, each of them with coins of varying ages and sizes. A Queen Elizabeth Jubilee silver dollar. An 1885 Liberty nickel. A 1943 American steel cent. Almost every pocket is taken.

Georgia swipes the loonie from the counter.

It's yours, she says. She drops the loonie in his hand. He smiles and turns to Ryan.

I'll take a pack of Winstons. I'll buy hers as well.

Georgia follows the man outside. Each of them lights a cigarette. The two wisps of smoke dance with one another before disappearing into the hot, thick air.

It's weird to see a priest outside of church, Georgia thinks. Like seeing your grade four teacher arguing with her boyfriend in the meat aisle at IGA, clutching a discounted chicken breast so hard that her fingers break through the saran wrap.

Georgia has only been to church a handful of times in her life, as Elsie didn't grow up particularly religious, but she was baptized into the Anglican Church as a baby. She knows this because there are photos of the event, of her in a white lace dress that touched the floor. Her mother still had her natural hair, mousey brown and down past her waist. She sheared it off with kitchen scissors and box-bleached it to a honey-blond shortly after Georgia's baptism, and she kept it that way for all of Georgia's childhood.

Georgia was ten when she started to notice the physical differences between herself and her mother. Elsie was almost six feet tall but slender. Little wrists and boney fingers.

All collarbones and elbows and hooked nose. Georgia was what her mother called *rosy*: round cheeks with dimples, full arms and thighs. Much shorter. She got her first period at nine and had to start wearing a bra that same year. Dark brown hair. In middle school, Georgia's male teachers gave her sweaters from the lost and found to cover her chest. She was somehow failing at womanhood, and thought that maybe looking more like her mother would help the situation. Most of Georgia's hair fell out the first time she lightened her hair with her mom's Blue Powder Bleach, but it grew back. Slowly, bleaching every six to eight weeks, Georgia got better at the multi-step process. She hasn't let her brown roots grow out more than an inch since then.

In one of the baptism photos, Elsie stands beside the Bloom twins, who she lived with when Georgia was a baby. Light blond curls and wrinkled white clothes. Their hair was naturally lighter than most, and their bodies were blurs of bright light overexposed by the camera's flash. The first time Georgia saw the photograph at age six, she asked Elsie, Are they angels?

And suddenly, Georgia realizes where she knows the priest from. The man smoking beside her is Arlo Bloom.

He is older by twenty years, but it is him—Georgia is sure of it. And she opens her mouth to tell him that she didn't recognize him at first, but he speaks before her lips can form the words.

Do you ever feel like no one could ever love you? he asks. As though you are just...unlovable?

Georgia blinks. Tourists often vent to her. They tell her the things that they can't tell anyone else. They save their secrets for summer trips because it is much easier to show all of yourself to another person if you are confident that

23

you will never see that person again. A confessional of sorts.

But Arlo Bloom is not a tourist. He's from here, if Georgia remembers correctly. You can't be a tourist in the place you were born.

It's clear, though, that he doesn't recognize Georgia. I guess it makes sense, she thinks. It's been twenty years since he saw her last. She is not that two-year-old brunette in butter-yellow overalls and Winnie the Pooh pull-ups. She is a grown woman. A woman who knows what she wants.

Yeah. I feel like that a lot, she says. Do you?

Arlo nods. He gazes at something far off, transfixed.

I often tell people that we do not have to prove ourselves through our works, he says. That, even though we may not be lovable, God loves us anyway.

You believe that?

Sure. Sometimes.

Not all the time? Georgia asks.

Sometimes I try to make myself more lovable anyway, Arlo says. By being better. Gentler. Not letting my anger get the best of me, that sort of thing.

What about other times?

Arlo chuckles.

Other times I'm less than gentle.

He glances at Georgia's bare feet. He savours his cigarette, only taking one puff every few minutes. Georgia finishes hers and lights another.

Where are you staying? she asks.

Arlo laughs again—a smoky laugh that becomes a cough.

The Super 8 off the service road. The movers aren't bringing the beds to the vicarage until tomorrow.

You're moving here? Tonight?

Tomorrow, yes. A job offer.

He takes a drag. Blows smoke.

I grew up here, and I hated it, and I left, and I said I would never come back, and then I did. A shitty odyssey. I can't tell if that's serendipitous or just very, very sad.

Pathetic is maybe the word I would use. Georgia smiles.

Arlo raises an eyebrow, but breaks into a matching smile.

Not everyone enjoys degradation, he says. Though I'm getting the sense that you might.

Would you like to find out?

Arlo nods.

Yes, he says. But not tonight. Tonight I'd like to offer you a ride home.

Alright.

Georgia follows Arlo across the street to the parking meter, to his maroon Dodge Grand Caravan with sliding doors. The inside of the van smells strongly of incense, and there are books piled on the back seats—tumbling over one another, falling to the car floor—and wax-lined coffee cups, and empty cigarette cartons, and white taper candles.

He drives terribly, speeding and swerving and steering with one hand and changing lanes without warning. His BlackBerry vibrates atop the centre console while he drives, again and again, and he sighs, but ignores it. Georgia feels brave. She picks it up.

You have a message from Zi, Georgia says. *Trinity letter. Haven't opened it yet.*

Anger flickers across Arlo's face for less than a second—a glitch in a television screen—and then it is gone. Georgia would like to see more of it.

Thank you, he mutters. You don't need to answer.

Who is Zi?

My son. Isaiah, Arlo says. He's with my wife.

Georgia feels her heart rate rise. Both in guilt and excitement.

What's your wife's name?

You don't want to know *my* name first? Arlo asks.

You should really watch where you're driving.

I could get to John Street blindfolded.

Does your wife enjoy watching you drive blindfolded?

Watching me fuck other women is more her thing, he says nonchalantly.

Georgia laughs, but Arlo's expression doesn't change. A minute passes before he speaks again.

I find you very attractive, and I'm sure that she would as well, but I would understand if you weren't interested. Not everyone's cup of tea.

Arlo drives down Elizabeth Street, past the public library, where the houses are new but empty. *FOR SALE* signs stand tall in dark lush lawns. No one is buying these days. He takes a left on John. Georgia's street has two apartment complexes and five foreclosed townhouses, three of which have smashed windows and boarded-up doors. Bike frames chained to racks, stripped of their seats. The air on John Street smells like dryer lint.

Elsie and Georgia live on the ground floor of a duplex with yellow siding. The grass out front is long and filled with ragweed and yellow dandelions. There's a pile of broken things on the right side of the house: a rusted barbecue; an old pink dollhouse filled with ants and grubs; a lawnmower; three twin-sized mattresses, stained and stacked atop one another; two halves of a Ping-Pong table; empty bird feeders; ripped canvases; a tricycle with no wheels.

It's the yellow one on the left, Georgia says.

I know, Arlo says.

He slows to a stop. Pulls back his parking brake.

The shade is called French Butter, he says. It was between that and a heinous swampy green that your mother liked. Her landlord—Reuben, like the sandwich—said she could only paint the house if she painted his parents' house in Hamilton too. For free. My sister and I helped her with both places, and you slurped up several handfuls of paint from one of the cans when none of us were looking, and we took you to the urgent care at St. Cecilia's to get your stomach pumped, but you threw up bright yellow all over me and Rose and your mother and the taxi seats on our way there, and then you felt better, and you started laughing and talking and asking Elsie those odd questions you always used to ask. What is the moon's name? Are you alive? Am I alive? Would you still love me if I was the moon?

Georgia is suddenly too warm. Flushed with disgust at herself. Stupid. You're so fucking stupid.

I'm sorry, she mutters.

But Arlo reaches an arm across the centre console and cups her chin in his hand, tilting her head back up to look at him, and kisses her. Once. The kiss is firm. Deep enough to feel his tongue on her teeth, and to taste his Winston cigarettes.

When he pulls away, he looks at her oddly. Not with an expression of desire, or anger, or sadness. It is a look that Georgia has seen before. On other lovers. On Mark. *Guilt.*

Somehow, it always happens like this. Georgia is twenty-two and as beautiful as she has ever been and as beautiful as she is ever going to be and as lovable as she is ever going to be, and here, now, she is not lovable at all.

Sleep well, Georgia, Arlo says.

AUGUST 2008

Isaiah Abel Bloom lets his mother lie to him about his university admissions results. He has applied to the undergraduate theological studies program at Trinity College in Toronto three times, at the request of his father. Each time he receives mail from the faculty, his mother, Felicity, opens the letter for him. She reads him the results so as to lessen the blow. All three applications have led to rejections. So she says.

Tonight, he sits on the green carpeted floor of a Super 8 hotel room as his mother opens his winter term admissions status letter. The two of them are boxed in by yellow floral wallpaper. Two double beds with yellow sheets and pillowcases. Two dark wood bedside tables, each with a lamp and a cordless phone. Glass-top desk. Wooden dresser. Mini-fridge of alcohol, pay as you drink.

Large suitcases and carry-ons are piled in front of the desk. The moving company packed most of the Blooms' possessions from the St. Andrew's Rectory in Minden into a transport truck, but Isaiah's father, Arlo, insisted that the family keep *valuables* with them in the car, and subsequently, in their hotel room.

Bloom Family Valuables

- Thirteen copies of the 1962 edition of the Anglican Church of Canada's *Book of Common Prayer*

- A coin collection, part of which is kept on Arlo's person

- All of Arlo's clothes

- All of Arlo's shoes

- All of Arlo's books

Isaiah received less than a week's notice before the move. St. Andrew's was never a parish with much money or community support, but the lifeline of diocesan grants dried up earlier that year, and the property value of the chapel—built in 1904—plummeted. There was talk that St. Andrew's might have to amalgamate with the closest Anglican church, which was a forty-five-minute drive away. Arlo would have had to serve as an associate priest, sharing duties with several other priests. He would have preached one third of the time. Every decision would have been a compromise.

Isaiah found out that his father had gotten the position at St. Paul's in Port Peter at the same time as the rest of the parish: during Arlo's last Sunday sermon at St. Andrew's. At dinner that evening, Felicity asked Arlo why the three of them needed to leave so quickly, after almost two decades in Minden.

Does it matter? Arlo asked. Isaiah is out of high school.

Isaiah was home-schooled.

He doesn't have a job he needs to quit.

Isaiah was never allowed to get a job, as it might've interfered with his church involvement.

He doesn't even have any friends here.

That was true.

Felicity Bloom carefully slices the envelope open with a house key. She has a head of dark brown hair, ironed flat, sharply cut at her chin. Chestnut eyes and black clothes—turtleneck and pencil skirt and stockings and Mary Janes. A bronze locket, with a little blue bird, midflight, hanging from a worn silver chain.

Isaiah is often told that he looks like his mother. The same hair and eyes. Only those within less than a foot of him can see his father's freckles spread over his nose and cheeks.

Felicity takes a folded piece of paper out of the envelope. Her eyes scan the page. She forces a frown.

I'm sorry, she lies.

Isaiah bites his bottom lip to keep from smiling.

It's okay, he says. Next year. Right?

Felicity gives her son a weak smile.

Of course, she says.

This is the only way that Isaiah can avoid going to seminary. With each rejection comes an exhale of relief—a little more time before he becomes a priest.

When Arlo talked about his only son to other members of the St. Andrew's parish up north in Minden, he never failed to mention that Isaiah had always wanted to be a priest. He used to preach to his stuffed animals, Arlo said. He'd write sermons in crayon and stand atop his bed as if he were at the pulpit. The congregants laughed, and Arlo laughed. They called it the most precious thing they'd ever heard.

It was a lie, predicated on a half-truth. Isaiah *did* write pages and pages of text as a child. He *did* set up his collection of Beanie Babies in rows on his bedroom floor, and stand on his twin-sized bed, and read to them. But he did not write sermons; he wrote poems. Poems about creating never-before-discovered colours with his friend Marianne at sleepaway Bible camp, and about the frothing Minden River's yellowy flotsam and jetsam in the summertime, and about how believing in God was easier than not believing in God because Isaiah would rather face an afterlife of pain than an afterlife of nothing at all.

Isaiah didn't think that he would live to be sixteen, let alone nineteen. Now, each minute of his life feels like another that he doesn't deserve. A life that must be improvised, because it includes an adulthood that he never gave much thought to. How does anyone know what they want to do with the rest of their life? How are they sure?

When a child lives in a perpetual cycle of discomfort and self-soothing, there is no future other than the immediate. Isaiah has not thought about how he might want to live his life as an adult because for almost two decades, he has had one focus: trying to quiet the birds in his head.

The cardinal is plump and vibrant red, with black feathers around its eyes and beak, and its song sounds like a child's cries, high in pitch, the blubbering incomprehensible. The cardinal was Isaiah's first bird. It arrived the first time his father hit him. The second time, a hummingbird joined in. Every time Isaiah's father lays a hand on him, Isaiah gets another bird. Now there are many, many birds.

Which Birds In Isaiah's Head Are The Loudest?

- The cardinal. Arrived when Isaiah was three years old. A red handprint on his face after spilling apple juice on his father's sermon. Birdsong like the sound of crying.

- The chickadee. Arrived when Isaiah was ten. Hands gripped tight around his throat, cutting off air, after packing a bag of his things and running away to live in the woods for an afternoon. Birdsong like wheezing.

- The crane. Arrived when Isaiah was sixteen, shortly after having sex at sleepaway Bible camp. Both wrists broken. Birdsong like a camp hymn. He's got the whole world in His hands.

- The hummingbirds. Hundreds. Maybe thousands. Isaiah cannot be sure. They arrive so often that Isaiah can't keep track. Almost every day. No singing. Just flapping. A kind of white noise.

Answer: All of the above.

The birds were much louder when Isaiah was a teenager. Once, the cardinal's cry was so painful that it woke him up at three a.m. The sound drilled into his temples and teeth. He left the vicarage, still in his pyjamas, walked until he reached the widest section of the Minden River across town, where the water was warm and calm, and kept walking until the water was waist-deep, and his feet found rocks and sticks and plants. He dove below the surface to feel the water on his face and hair, and he swam in circles until he felt brave enough to approach the main current of the river. It roared. The speed of the water carried fallen tree branches fast enough to crack them against boulders. Isaiah waited for a slight lull, patiently. Almost. Almost. Now.

Trying to fight the current's direction would have been a dangerous game, so Isaiah let his body go limp, and he floated at a remarkable speed, as though he was one of the pine branches. The water splashed up and into his mouth and eyes. It was impossible to see where he was going, or what obstacles he needed to avoid. But he trusted that the water knew what was best. The water would take him where he was meant to go.

The current changed, and Isaiah was suddenly underwater, tensing every muscle in his body. This displeased the water, and it twisted his limbs violently, flipped him over, upside-down, the crown of his head on the riverbed, and the birds flapped and screamed, and he gained speed, forward, forward, and a rock, a hard smash against his temple, and he was everywhere, tasting dirt, tasting algae, tasting blood, no up, no out, no air, no deciding what his last thought would be, who he would pray for, whose face he would picture in his mind before he left this earth, and he was not certain that this was what he wanted, to leave the world like this, he just wanted the birds to be quiet, he was just so desperate for silence, but he didn't want to die there, then, not like that, and as if God Himself was listening, Isaiah's pyjama shirt snagged on a root. Keeping him in place. Alive. While the river charged forward.

Arlo Bloom hugged every doctor and nurse in the Minden ER. He lauded them for saving his son's life. I just couldn't live with myself if anything happened to my boy, he told one nurse. He leaned in close to Isaiah as the nurse left the examination room.

You're fucking dead, he whispered.

Isaiah is nineteen now, and it is easier to keep the birds quiet. Walking along the Minden riverbank until his feet are blistered. Reading and rereading his favourite poetry book: *Glass, Irony & God* by Anne Carson. Praying his daily office alone. His head is never truly silent, but with patience, he can calm his birds and himself to a baseline.

Isaiah and Felicity are still on the hotel room floor when Arlo returns. He massages his temples and walks to where his wife is sitting and kisses her on the crown of her head.

I thought you two would be sleeping, he says.

I picked up the mail from the new vicarage, Felicity says, yawning. A few things for you. The Trinity letter.

And?

A rejection. Another one.

Arlo throws his leather satchel onto the glass-top desk, muttering to himself. Fucking ridiculous.

Felicity stands and begins to get ready for bed, but Isaiah freezes, watching his father move around the hotel room. He listens closely to the cadence of Arlo's breath. Isaiah is a player in a perpetual game that he never agreed to play. The game involves paying close attention to his father's tone of voice and how hard he picks up objects and how hard he places those objects back down and how he flexes his fingers, and watching for any potential triggers to his father's anger like mugs left unwashed or music set too loud or music set too quiet or the TV remote in the wrong place, and anticipating other triggers that he's unable to control like time of day and time of year and time of pay cycle and weather and whether it is a holiday, and the game is exhausting and Isaiah Abel Bloom is not meant to win. He will never win. If he plays the game perfectly, he might be able to identify whether he is in a situation that will result in his harm. The problem is that sometimes, there is nothing wrong, and he is hurt anyway.

Did you have a good time? Isaiah asks.

His voice cracks. Arlo's eyes narrow.

Pardon me?

I—you were out. Outside, in town. I just meant did you have a good time while you were. Out. Side.

A good time?

Isaiah looks to his mother, but her gaze is fixed on a stack of sheet music in her lap. The flapping at the back of his brain makes it difficult to concentrate.

Sorry, Isaiah says. I'm sorry.

Did you move this? Arlo asks, opening a cardboard moving box.

I just—they were on the balcony, Isaiah stammers. I thought you might want everything together.

The 1967 commemorative RCM mint set goes on top here. The Alex Colville.

I didn't touch them.

You just said that you moved the fucking box.

Yes, Arlo, he hid the coins on purpose, Felicity says. Everything he does is spiritual warfare against you.

Arlo's expression shifts. Brows low, eyes narrow, every muscle in his face taut.

This is Felicity Bloom's way of protecting her son. A cruel comment, or two, or as many as it takes to divert Arlo's attention away from Isaiah and onto her instead. It is not foolproof. It prolongs the inevitable.

I think that Isaiah and I should discuss this privately, Arlo says.

He walks to the other end of the hotel room and opens the sliding door to the balcony. Motions for Isaiah to follow him.

The outside air is colder than Isaiah expects. The hotel balcony overlooks Lake Ligeia, larger than the modest lakes Isaiah is used to up north in Minden. It is so dark out that the lake looks black, and Isaiah cannot see where the water ends and the night sky begins.

The door to the balcony is made of clear glass, and when Arlo closes and locks it, he and Isaiah stand perfectly in Felicity's line of sight. She is perched on the end of one of the double beds, watching, when Arlo backhands Isaiah. Hard.

Isaiah is not positive how many times his father strikes him. The cardinal is in his head, screaming. A new hummingbird, green and white with a crimson throat, seventy wingbeats per second, slams itself against Isaiah's skull, again and again. The cold concrete balcony floor. Arlo's face an inch from his own. You make me like this, he says. You push me to this point, and then I react, and I'm the bad guy. Felicity kneeling right on the other side of the sliding door, palms against the glass, inky streaks of mascara down her cheeks. Blood in Isaiah's mouth: Drink this, and be thankful.

Later, after Felicity has gone to bed, Arlo and Isaiah sit on the floor of the balcony together. Isaiah cradles a bucket of ice from the hotel ice machine between his knees, chewing the frozen chunks to numb his split lip and lower jaw. Arlo smokes half a pack of Winstons. Isaiah doesn't mind the smell of cigarette smoke. It is soothing, in a way. If his father is smoking, his father is calm.

Do you ever get bad dreams? Arlo asks.

Sometimes, Isaiah says.

About me?

Different things, Isaiah lies.

I had one last night, Arlo says.

About Aunt Roselyn?

Arlo nods.

We were building things out of wet sand, Arlo says. Small objects. Sewing needles and thimbles and thread. I looked up, and she was suddenly gone. Then I woke up. And there was quiet—the thick kind. The quiet was all around me.

Arlo's voice trails off. He is far away.

Isaiah wishes that he could put a hand atop his father's and comfort him without being afraid. He sits. He listens. It is the best he can do.

You know I love you, right? Arlo asks.

I know, Isaiah says.

Good, Arlo whispers. Good.

He sets his cigarette pack aside.

Have you prayed evensong yet tonight?

No.

Me neither.

He hands Isaiah a prayer book. Palms his own.

Isaiah runs his finger down the lectionary page to find the psalms appointed to the evening. Arlo officiates. Isaiah responds.

> O Lord, open thou our lips—
> And our mouth shall show forth thy praise.
> O God, make speed to save us.
> O Lord, make haste to help us.

Isaiah is grateful that morning and evening prayers have a set script, dictated by the day of the week and the time of the liturgical year. He finds freeform prayer difficult, when it is just him and God and he is expected to come up with the right things to say.

He feels a similar kind of calm when he serves as an acolyte for his father's masses. There are meant to be no gaps of silence between calls and responses, meaning that Isaiah's words always follow Arlo's as if they are part of the same sentence, spoken from the very same mouth. When Arlo moves the missal to one side of the altar, Isaiah always moves to the opposite side. Before Arlo pours his wine into the chalice, Isaiah holds a bowl of water and helps him to clean his hands. If there is any leftover wine or water or host in the chalice after Arlo is done, Isaiah must consume it himself. In any other circumstance, Isaiah struggles to connect with his father; here, he cannot possibly conceive of an instance in which he could be more connected to another human being.

His salvation is in his father's hands, connected through blood and ceremony. Fear and love are not two strands intertwined: they are the same strand, and Isaiah cannot distinguish one from the other.

AUGUST 2008

Prayer never came easily to Felicity Bloom. Her father, James Lovesee, told her when she was small that with enough practice, prayer would become as intuitive as breathing. Felicity never found anything intuitive—not even breathing. Every waking moment of her life contained thousands of commands from her head to the rest of her body, willing her to be a person.

Felicity spent her childhood uncomfortable on land, preferring to inhabit the water. Every childhood memory bore the scent of algae—hair always dripping wet at mass, church shoes soaked and dress wrinkled as she sang in the choir. She arrived at parish events looking like a sea creature, ruining James Lovesee's facade of Anglo-Catholic tidiness.

James Lovesee was an assistant librarian at the Minden Public Library, but did not want to appear as such. When his daughter began singing at St. Andrew's, he coached her to tell the other parishioners that he worked as a spiritual director. He packed up his poetry books and pagan history volumes and replaced them with theology textbooks. He stopped scavenging herbs for remedies and told Felicity that she was never to leave her tarot card deck out for others to see. The congregation must think we are one of them, he told Felicity. They'll accept us as one of their own. We'll make other Christian friends with Christian jobs who live in beautiful houses in the winter and massive cottages in the summer, and one of them will be your husband or wife.

She did not understand what it was about growing and drying herbs for ointments that was so embarrassing, or what the problem was with her cards. She liked running ritual baths with rose petals and honey and milk powder on Imbolc and jumping over the firepit in her bare feet on the night of summer solstice. She loved nature and all it had to offer. She loved the water most of all, though it did not always love her back.

Luckily, Felicity Bloom did not need to rely on her own faculties to get her through a life of performance. She had a bird nested in her skull, who told her what to do.

Felicity thinks that the bird is a mourning dove. The cooing of mourning doves is the closest thing she can find to the sound her head bird makes. She can often hear it singing. Sometimes it flaps its wings. Sometimes it pecks at her temples and gives her a headache.

The bird first made itself known to Felicity when she was five years old, still living with her father and grandfather in the old Port Peter lighthouse.

Felicity's grandfather would wake her from sleep while the sky was still dark to take her Bird hunting. He would help her into her yellow raincoat and rubber boots. He'd heat a beeswax candle over the stovetop until it was as soft and mouldable as bread dough, ripping the mass into four pieces: two for his own ears, and two for Felicity's. The wax wouldn't be hot enough to burn Felicity's ear canals, but would still be uncomfortably warm. He'd hold her hand, leading her down the spiral staircase of the lighthouse and out onto the wet grass of the cliffside.

Before Felicity was born, her grandfather had rigged three traps in the sand. They were large nets, triggered to fall by someone walking into fishing line pulled taut like trip wire. Sometimes, when Felicity and her grandfather went to check the nets, there would be skunks and racoons and groundhogs in them. Once he found a baby deer, trapped with its lanky legs poked through gaps in the netting, flailing for who knows how long. As exciting as it was to catch something large, Felicity's grandfather freed the fawn immediately. It doesn't deserve to die, he said.

One night, a Bird got tangled in one of the nets. It was young. Its long blond curls were knotted. Tiny fingers gripped at the wet sand through the mesh. Tears spilt down its fear-stricken face. The Bird sang, but Felicity could not hear the words. She could only discern the rising and falling tone, gently tugging her awareness away from the present, back into the recesses of her mind. She felt woozy.

Felicity's grandfather removed his hunting knife from its leather sheath, got down on his knees in the sand, and pressed the net down to keep the Bird still. It was speaking—pleading, most likely.

Felicity's grandfather positioned the blade at the top of the Bird's neck, just below its chin. The Bird squirmed. It kicked sand up into his eyes.

Then the Bird noticed Felicity, standing a little way off, and the two of them locked eyes. The Bird calmed, lying perfectly still beneath the net, no longer struggling, breathing slowly, and looking at Felicity with a kind of trust, as if sure she would protect it. Felicity felt this trust, though she couldn't explain how. Compassion overwhelmed her tiny body like a great flood. She moved to take the wax out of her ears.

And Felicity's grandfather slit the Bird's throat.

The Bird had expected Felicity to help, hadn't it?

A flapping began behind Felicity's eyes, then—deep in her head. It startled her. Then, a voice.

You are only worth what you can remember.

Felicity did not hear the voice again until she was newly seventeen, the day she caught Arlo's twin sister, Roselyn, getting drunk off communion wine in the St. Andrew's sacristy.

I guess you're going to tell Father Warren, Roselyn said. And my brother.

Felicity shook her head. She helped Roselyn up to a sitting position on the floor.

Can I, um, pray for you? Felicity asked.

Not sure what good it'll do at this point, Roselyn said.

Felicity sat cross-legged, gently taking Roselyn's hands in her own. The two of them looked less like they were praying, and more like they were holding a seance.

Heavenly Father, Felicity said. I, Felicity Lovesee, come before you today with a humble heart, asking for mercy and aid on behalf of your daughter Roselyn Bloom, a child of salt and light who has fallen from your grace. Lord God, please draw your dear Roselyn back into your loving embrace. Please forgive her for all she has done and all she has failed to do.

Felicity opened her eyes. Before now, she had experienced Roselyn at a distance, singing in the choir while Roselyn played the organ up in the loft. They had spoken before, of course, at various parish functions, but always in a group of other parishioners and choristers and servers. She knew that Roselyn and her twin brother had grown up in Port Peter, where Felicity was born, and moved to Minden together after Arlo finished seminary. She knew that Roselyn was an excellent organist, particularly when it came to

Early-Renaissance mass settings. But she had never really given any thought to the grey of her eyes or the bump in her nose or the little gap between her two front teeth. Groups of her freckles spread out like points on a map. The curls in her white-blond hair, some coiled tight, others falling loose and straightening out at the ends. Felicity was taking in these details, mesmerized and curious, when Roselyn began to kiss her. She began to kiss Roselyn back, and the whole world, everything except that terrifying, sacred space, fell away. Felicity held Roselyn's bronze locket in her hand. She ran her thumb over the blue bird.

That's when the mourning dove spoke once again. The same phrase as before.

You are only worth what you can remember.

Roselyn and Felicity began to meet in secret. Roselyn's brother, Arlo, lied to Father Warren about the girls' whereabouts, standing guard at the chapel doors while Roselyn and Felicity met in the organ loft. This small mercy gave them the time they needed.

Their time together was treated as a desperate, primal rush, tinged with the fear that someone could catch them at any time. They clamped sweaty hands over one another's mouths, glancing at the top of the stairs to the loft, ears pricked like those of a cat on guard. Roselyn left love bites high on the insides of Felicity's thighs. She twisted and arched her delicate pianist's fingers inside Felicity as if she were playing a hymn. Each meeting was nothing less than paradise on earth.

One morning after mass, Roselyn pulled Felicity aside in the hallway leading to the parish hall.

Open your hand, she told her.

Felicity did. Roselyn pressed her bird locket into Felicity's palm, the chain dangling high above the ground.

I don't understand, Felicity said. Why are you giving me this?

So that you always have a piece of me, Roselyn said. Wherever you go. Whoever you become.

Arlo Bloom found his twin sister's body at the mouth of the Minden River two days later. No note. He did not participate in her requiem mass, nor did he attend the visitation in the parish hall or the burial in the St. Andrew's churchyard. He did not leave the vicarage for an entire week.

After the burial, Felicity approached the vicarage door in a black dress and lace mantilla veil. She knocked twice. Waited.

Ten minutes passed before Arlo Bloom opened the door. Purple bags below his eyes. Unshaven—blond curls wild and unkempt. White T-shirt stained with sweat.

What do you want? he slurred.

Felicity could smell the wine, strong on his breath.

The service was beautiful, she said. I wanted you to know. It was lovely. We sang—

Do you know what it feels like to die, Felicity? Arlo asked.

No, she said. I don't.

Roselyn and I were one fucking person, Arlo said. And now we're dead.

Arlo. You're still here.

Arlo shook his head.

Felicity reached forward, hesitantly, and took Arlo's hands in her own.

Look at me, she whispered. I loved your sister. Very much. And I know that you feel the same way. If you're dead, I'm dead with you. We're dead together. You don't have to suffer alone.

Grief is a merciless matchmaker. When two people fall in love after loss, they are desperate to hang on to whatever morsel of the dead they can get their hands on. At first, it feels safe to find that morsel in someone who has been left behind. But it will not last. It isn't real. They fall in love with details—aspects of their dead loved one that they recognize. Facial features, speech patterns. They fall in love with having their sadness seen and heard. A person who is grieving can love and be loved in a healthy, beautiful way, but when two parties build the house of their love upon a foundation of bones, when they love each other because they cannot leave each other, that is where the trouble starts.

Isaiah Abel Bloom was conceived on the night of his aunt's funeral. A product of mourning, marked by death before he was even born.

Felicity has built up a garden wall in her mind that separates Roselyn from her everyday thoughts. When Felicity is helping serve breakfast at St. Andrew's or running a charity drive or clipping coupons for groceries, Roselyn doesn't exist. She cannot exist. But every night, when her husband has fallen asleep, Felicity puts all her other thoughts to bed, hoisting herself over the garden wall, allowing herself to lie in her Roselyn memories as if they are packing snow, forming around the shape of her body, encasing her in a pleasurable cold. And after an hour or so of this, she will leave. Lying in the snow too long could kill her.

The St. Paul's vicarage in Port Peter is a two-storey townhouse with white siding, a black tiled roof, and black window frames. A small, sloping roof hangs over a front porch with white pillars, a white railing, and a metal-framed porch swing with a floral green cushion. The mailbox is tin, fixed to the wall. A wooden crucifix sits on the door hanger where a knocker would normally be. A pair of metal numbers, *84*, are nailed into the siding above the door.

Felicity is most interested in the backyard. She goes there first, while Isaiah unpacks his cardboard boxes and blue Rubbermaid bins in the attic. Arlo is directing the movers downstairs. The front and back yards are both rectangular, perfect reflections of each other, connected by a thin walkway of cracked concrete stones. Black garbage bins on wheels and a hose. The backyard is overgrown. A lawnmower sits in the middle of the lawn, rusted and hidden in the tall grass. It looks as though it is part of the landscape—as if the landscape has reclaimed it. Ragweed, dandelion, pods of yellow mushrooms on tree stumps, wild raspberry, a patch of mint at the base of a little garden shed.

The vicarage is at the top of a hill—a fact only obvious when one is in the backyard. At the very back edge of the lawn, the terrain begins to slope. Rotting two-by-fours become steps. In Port Peter, the beach sand is rocks and barbecue coals and plastic water bottles and glass beer bottles and candy wrappers and condom wrappers and hard French fries that the seagulls can't find and a small amount of dirt-brown sand, dark like molasses.

Lake Ligeia is difficult for Felicity to read. She was born in Port Peter, like Arlo, but moved to Minden with her father when she was nearing six years old. She only spent a small fraction of her early life here, around this odd body of water. Her childhood memories of the lake are merely flashes of sensation. The smell of rotting fish. The smoothness of green beach glass, old pieces of beer bottles softened by the waves. The grey of her grandfather's beard. The blood of the Bird, throat slit, soaking into the sand.

Now she is back, and Lake Ligeia is still a mystery.

The wooden steps begin to creak. Felicity turns. Arlo Bloom descends the hill and walks through the sand to meet her.

Enjoying the ambiance?

Felicity nods, mulling over her words.

You seem to be in better spirits than you were last night, she says finally.

Do not dwell on the past, Arlo says. See, I am doing a new thing.

I don't see anything.

Felicity.

He's your height now.

Pardon?

Isaiah. He is as tall as you.

Arlo shakes his head.

He is shorter than me. By a few inches at least.

He isn't.

It's his boots, then. Those brown ones he wears. They add height.

Felicity pauses.

He could hit you back, Arlo.

Fear crosses Arlo's face. Felicity catches it before indifference takes its place.

And I could kill him, *Felicity*, Arlo says calmly, lighting a cigarette. Or he could kill you. Or you could kill me. Or anyone could kill anyone else, if they wanted to. And then there would be no one left to hear your melodramatic fucking grandstanding.

He takes a drag. Blows smoke.

You'll understand when you're older, he adds.

Felicity was seventeen and still living with her father in Minden when she became pregnant with Isaiah. Arlo was thirty-two at the time, serving as an associate priest at St. Andrew's. They married before Felicity was even showing. She never got her driver's licence—Arlo insisted he could be the one who drove. She has never had her own bank account. Never lived on her own. Never booked her own doctor's or dentist's appointments.

These differences did not matter until the two of them started arguing, and then they mattered more than anything else in the world. It was his life experience up against hers. His car. His job. His last name. What could she do? *Leave?* How?

Arlo lights another cigarette.

I met a woman last night. At the convenience store.

Did you, Felicity says. She doesn't frame it like a question.

I think that you would like her, Arlo says.

You mean for—

Yes.

Silence. Arlo sighs.

Forget it, Flick, he says. I'll leave you to continue your conversation with the water.

We are barely moved in, Felicity says. We *just* arrived.

I didn't go out intending to find someone.

A happy accident, then, Felicity spits. Good for you. I'm happy for you.

Arlo's face is a dark shade of red. If they were in the house, he would likely hit something. The wall. A table. But here, there is nothing for him to hit but Felicity. She would be lying if she said it hadn't happened before.

You asked me to do this, he says. *You're* the one who had the idea. *You* said that *this* was what you wanted.

Felicity is silent. Sex with her husband feels like several acts in isolation, separate from her emotional attachment to him. Felicity loves Arlo. Felicity finds Arlo attractive. Arlo knows what it is she likes—to feel in control. To be the one in power. This makes her body respond. And all these things, together, should make Felicity happy and satisfied. But they don't. It is as if her love for Arlo, and Arlo's acts upon her body, and her body's eventual climax, are unrelated entities.

What can I do? he asked, nineteen years in, when she could no longer come under his touch. What do you want me to do?

Her answer was one that surprised them both. She didn't want him to do anything to her at all—she wanted to watch him with another woman. At least, she thought that was what she wanted. That must be it. That would solve the disconnect.

Arlo takes one of her hands and holds it between both of his own.

I want what you want, he says. Always. I just need you to tell me what that is.

I just want to get settled, first, Felicity says. And I want you to extend some mercy. To your son.

Arlo nods. He leans forward and presses his forehead against hers. But Felicity isn't looking at him anymore. She is looking across the water.

Can you hear it?

The movers will be finished soon, Arlo says.

Felicity is fixated on a point that Arlo cannot see. Her eyes narrowed. Her lips pursed into a frown.

Flick, Arlo says. Hey. Felicity.

You don't hear it? Felicity asks.

Arlo quiets. He hears seagulls farther down the beach. Wind rustling the pine branches. Lake water sloshing against the shore.

Hear what?

The singing.

Arlo looks out at the water, then back at his wife.

We should finish unpacking, he says.

He grabs her wrist and begins to walk towards the make-shift steps, back up the hill.

An urge presents itself, suddenly, to Felicity. To break away from her husband and go back to the edge of the water. Into the water. Across the water. If she could swim far enough, maybe she could hear the singing better. Maybe she could make out the words.

AUGUST 1970

The Birds do not lure pregnant Port Peter women to the cliffside on purpose. We are radiant and ravenous creatures, but we are not cruel. The Birds only sing for each other. The Birds sing to bring lost Birds back home.

What Does a Bird Song Sound Like To Another Bird?

- Wind through willow branches and words of comfort: You are loved. You are everything you need to be right now.

- The trickle of creek water deep in the woods and beautiful, convincing lies: You are not safe out there. You are only safe here, with us.

- The cracks and pops of bonfire wood and violent threats— empty, of course: We will be angry if you are not back by nightfall. We will pluck out your feathers one by one. We will carve out a tree and keep you inside it for the rest of time.

Answer: Every Bird hears something different.
They hear whatever they need.

We do not all look the same. One of us has beady blue eyes and thin lips and a square jaw and size-fourteen feet. Another has big hands and short black hair and stretch marks up her thighs like lightning strikes. Some Birds have small white feathers from their wrists to their shoulders. Some of us have five feathers total, long and black, sticking out from our backs. Some Birds have no feathers at all. We do not need to use our looks as a means to an end. We need only use our voice.

The Birds live a mostly pleasant existence. We eat fresh plump peaches until we are too full to move, and we lie naked in the cliffside grass with our bulging bellies baking in the sun. We swim in Lake Ligeia until our fingers wrinkle and our muscles ache, and we forget what it is to be on dry land. Each day is a holy, holy thing.

We are born without names. We can choose a name when we find one that we like. We can change it if we find one that suits us better.

One Bird prefers not to choose a name. She doesn't want one. She has fine blond hair down past her hip bones and black eyes and seven moles scattered across her face. She has an overbite and webbed toes. She cannot think of any name in all of history that would suit her features. Her mother and sisters and aunts and cousins and friends have names. They bother the Bird about her namelessness often. They tell her that at some point, she will have to choose a name.

What will your legacy be if you have no name? her friend Lila asks. How will the other Birds remember you?

I don't want to be remembered, the Bird says.

Lila laughs. It is a loud laugh—one that turns to wheezing, drowning in open air.

We all want to be remembered, she says.

The Bird without a name enjoys being alone. While the others swim in the lake below, she sits on the cliffside, her legs dangling over the edge. She sings quietly. She sings for herself.

She doesn't see the young man emerge from the wooded trail until he is already standing beside her. He has thick black rubber boots and tan cargo pants and a bright yellow raincoat like a sunflower. A wiry black beard with bare patches.

The Bird freezes. She thinks that, perhaps, if she is perfectly still, she will blend in with the landscape. She closes her eyes.

When she opens them up, the man is still there.

Were you the one singing? he asks.

The Bird scrunches her face.

You could hear me?

The man nods.

All the way from the lighthouse, he says. My name is James Lovesee.

A pause. It takes the Bird a moment to figure out that the man is waiting for her to say her own name.

I'm—um, she stammers. I'm—my name is—

And she settles on the very first word to pop into her mind.

Kind, she says. I'm Kind. My name—my name is Kind.

James raises an eyebrow.

Your parents named you *Kind*?

Mm-hmm, Kind says. They...like...adjectives.

And are you?

Am I what?

Are *you* kind?

I guess that's for other people to decide, she says.

James smiles. One of his incisors is missing.

Do you live in town? he asks.

Yes, Kind lies. By the water.

And what are you doing all the way out here by yourself? James asks.

I was...watching the Birds, she says.

Kind points at the group of Birds laughing and splashing in the lake below.

James sits down on the grass beside Kind. He places a hand above his eyes to shield them from the sun as he looks over the cliffs.

Those girls—they aren't girls? he asks.

No, Kind says. Not really.

How can you live so close to them? Aren't you afraid they'll kill you?

They're harmless, Kind says, now feeling odd. They're like us.

James shakes his head, but he does not push the subject any further.

Have you ever been to the top of a lighthouse before? he asks.

I've never been in any part of a lighthouse before, Kind says. Top. Bottom. Middle.

James laughs.

Come with me back to mine, he says. I'll show you every part.

He says it like it is an order—like there is no room for Kind to say no.

She looks at him. Back at the Birds in the water. Back at him.

Okay then, Kind says.

Okay then, James says.

Kind's eyes eat up the lighthouse interior. High ceiling. Stone floors beneath pale orange carpeting. Real stone walls. The beginning of a spiral staircase that curls straight up for what seems like forever. Dust on every shelf of the empty bookcase, on the little fold-out table, on the glass of the empty picture frames on the wall. A yellow floral couch. A thick canvas coat draped over a spindled kitchen chair, drying near the lit fireplace.

Massive wooden shelves with live bark edges run along the wall across from the couch. Each shelf holds a row of paperbacks, falling against one another like dominoes between the gaps where other books have been taken out.

Suddenly, James's hands are around Kind's waist—the very first time he touches her. His touch is confident, as if he has held her a thousand times before, like a husband would touch a wife. Like a man would grab something that belongs to him and only him. He cradles her hip bones in his palms, then pulls her body forward towards his own.

The lantern room is at the very top, James adds. My father won't be able to hear us.

Kind looks at James's body not with lust, but with genuine curiosity. Her eyes devour his features. She wants to explore him—all of him—although she isn't exactly sure what that might entail. She is certain that he knows, though. He seems like the kind of man who knows what to do.

She moves her face forward, hesitant, like when you hold a puzzle piece above the puzzle to see where it might fit. She kisses him lightly on the tip of his nose. His eyelids flutter.

Thank you, he says.

You're welcome, Kind says.

She kisses him again, for real this time. Mouth fully open. Wide. He does the same. Two whales swallowing each other—no Jonah. He keeps his mouth on hers and walks them back to the yellow pullout couch. She falls backwards onto it, him on top of her, the world on top of them both, pushing them together, gravity itself seemingly pulling him lower and lower until he is buried deep inside her.

She feels a sharp pain. Weight. The stick of sweat. The stink of man. It isn't desire, but need. In this moment, Kind's body needs to finish what it began. She pulls him closer. Grips him tight. Her fair hair in her face and in his mouth. The wood of the couch frame digging into her back. Farther. Farther. There. And again. And again. Inhale after inhale. Ripples of heat behind her eyes and in her toes. Again. Again. Then, a kind of fullness. Finished.

Kind expects to feel different. She feels the same, but sore.

A voice surfaces in her head, telling her it is time to come home. She feels woozy.

James climbs off her and starts to put his pants back on.

Did you... Did you have a good time? he asks.

I did, Kind says matter-of-factly. And now I would like to go home.

She puts her dress back on. James walks her out. When they reach the grass, she stops and turns.

I'm walking back by myself, Kind says.

Oh, James says. Did I do something wrong?

Kind shakes her head no. The voice inside her is louder now. The sound makes her eardrums ache.

You are beautiful, Kind says.

Not in the way that people normally say it.

To people, telling someone they are beautiful is a gesture done in love. It is a compliment. To Birds, it is an observation of danger. A fact. A warning.

Kind leans forward and kisses James on the tip of his nose for the second time. It is also the last time.

She walks back to the cliffside, where the Birds are lounging.

There you are, Lila says, picking sand out of her toenails. We were beginning to worry.

My name is Kind, Kind says firmly.

She tries to say it as confidently as she can, but she is still unsure. The name feels odd in her mouth, like it doesn't belong. How do you make a name fit? How do you know if it is the right one?

AUGUST 2008

St. Paul's is a destination church attended exclusively by city tourists and retirees from one town over who like to see the lake on their Sunday-morning outing. It is the church for people who pray that their kitchen renovations will go well.

Georgia and Elsie are late to the eleven o'clock service. It is Elsie's idea to go, sprung on Georgia at the last possible minute.

Didn't I tell you my old friend Arlo Bloom just moved back to town? Sorry, *Father* Bloom. He's the new priest at St. Paul's. You remember him, don't you? From when you were little? Sure you do. Georgia, don't make that face at me—you remember.

The St. Paul's parking lot is packed with white SUVs and sapphire-blue hybrids with fake eyelashes on the front headlights and cartoon family windshield stickers.

The chapel itself is Port Peter small but city fancy. Smooth cement steps lead up to a ten-foot-high arched black door with a brass knocker. Two large stained glass windows sit above the door, glinting red and blue and green and gold. They depict two scenes, neither of which Georgia recognizes. The left window shows the moment Saint Peter walks on water; the right window shows Jesus raising Lazarus from the dead.

Inside, the people of the congregation stand in their pews and recite a prayer in imperfect unison, some voices so off in their timing that it sounds as though they are singing a round. The air smells like Chanel No. 5 and wet wood. Georgia watches a kid in a suit too big for his body flick a smaller boy in the back of the head. Women with frilled sleeveless shirts and nude lipstick and tester perfume from The Bay shoot exasperated glances at their boring, balding husbands.

A lanky boy with black hair stands in the doorway. He smiles at Georgia and her mother, hands them each a white leaflet.

THE NINTH SUNDAY AFTER TRINITY
Sunday, August 4th
9:00 a.m.

ST. PAUL'S ANGLICAN CHURCH
PORT PETER

"Go in the strength you have."
Celebrant & Preacher

The Rev'd Fr. Arlo Bloom
Vicar, St. Paul's

The leaflet is thick like a double-feature magazine. It has weight in Georgia's hand.

The only empty pew is at the very front. Elsie folds out the wooden kneeler topped with a bright red cushion. The pew creaks as Georgia takes her place beside her mother. The two of them stand because the others are standing. This many people in the same room cannot *all* be incorrect, they think. Somebody had to have stood first.

When Georgia looks up from her leaflet, Arlo Bloom is standing at the altar with his back to the congregation. His blond hair is slicked back, not a curl out of place. He wears bright green robes with pink and yellow flowers embroidered on the back.

A woman with a dark bob stands in a black robe on the opposite side of the altar, and halfway through the prayer, she begins to sing.

> *Behold, God is my helper,*
> *the Lord is with them that uphold my soul—*

The woman's voice is radiant and haunting and angelic and bewitching. The power of it fills the chapel with sound. A fatigue washes over Georgia.

> *Glory be to the Father, and to the Son,*
> *and to the Holy Ghost:*
> *As it was in the beginning, is now,*
> *and ever shall be,*
> *world without end.*
> *Amen.*

Then, silence. Arlo turns and slowly walks to the pulpit.

Please be seated, he says.

Finally, instructions, Georgia thinks.

Just in case you're wondering, Father Bloom starts, yes, Bishop Marcelle bet his job to me in a game of bridge, and yes, I am, obviously, very good at bridge.

Laughter bubbles up in pockets across the congregation. Georgia doesn't laugh. She looks at Father Bloom—freckles, light eyes, smile lines—and feels her face get hot.

I'm very grateful that you're here today, he continues. Each and every one of you.

Arlo looks out beyond the pulpit. He catches sight of Elsie and smiles. When he sees Georgia sitting beside her, he tries and fails to keep from frowning.

A noticeable pause—a moment in which Arlo Bloom opens his mouth but cannot remember the words he is supposed to say.

Georgia looks at the leaflet in her lap. She feels Arlo's eyes on her, but doesn't look back up. The moment seems to stretch on, longer and longer, like taffy pulled at both ends.

Our, um, our Gospel today is from Matthew, Arlo finally continues.

The sermon is now in full swing. Georgia cannot hear what is being said. She cannot breathe. She cannot think.

She stands before the idea to stand even enters her brain. She doesn't look back at her mother before awkwardly stepping out of the pew and walking back down the aisle, towards the front door, away from the altar, from her mother, from Arlo. When she exits the chapel, she devours the outside air in big gulps. Inhale after inhale, higher and higher, until she is panicking, trying to catch breath that has sped ahead. She kicks off her shoes so hard that one of them tumbles down the steps onto the front path.

There is August heat and the reek of sweat and the relentless brightness beating down on her eyes from the blinding summer sun, and then there is vomit, erupting out of her onto the front steps of St. Paul's. It is the kind of vomiting that never seems to end, heave after heave, emptying herself of herself. She is on her hands and knees on the cement in front of the chapel door.

When she is finished, she looks up.

A young man about Georgia's age stands over her, wearing a cream-coloured cardigan too thick for August. Brown curly hair and dark eyes. Dimples. Freckles. A fat lip, and a bruise on one side of his mouth.

Georgia makes a face at him. He doesn't move. He just looks at her.

Fuck off, Georgia says. She wipes vomit off her chin with her sleeve.

The boy doesn't move.

Please, Georgia adds.

The boy pulls a small white package from his pants pocket.

I have wet wipes, he says quietly.

Georgia wipes her hands on her jumpsuit.

I'm good, thanks. Were you just walking by? And really like vomit?

I don't, he says. Like vomit, I mean. The act and the substance, both of them. I mean, neither.

He plays with his cuticles. Georgia sits up, wiping vomit off the ends of her hair.

I was in there before, he continues. Not that I was following you. I don't have a vomit fetish. That's one of my favourite qualities about myself, actually. I saw you come in, and I saw Elsie, your mom— I mean, your mom and my dad were friends when they were young, I've seen pictures, and you look like Elsie, do people tell you that? They must tell you that often, like, you have the same hair and cheeks. I wasn't looking at your cheeks though. Or hers. I don't have a cheek fetish either. No cheeks. Or vomit. Nothing. I don't think about anything during sex.

He's bright red.

I'm Isaiah Bloom, he says.

Right, Georgia says. Priest's kid.

Isaiah nods a little too hard.

I'm sorry. For following you. I just wanted to make sure you were okay.

I'm fucking fantastic, Georgia says.

She takes a carton of Benson & Hedges from her pocket. She offers a cigarette to Isaiah. He shakes his head furiously.

No death fetish either, Georgia muses. How endearing.

Memento mori, Isaiah says.

Georgia cocks her head.

Remember that you, uh, have to die, Isaiah clarifies. It's just a saying.

Georgia clears her throat. She spits the remaining bile in her mouth onto the step beside her.

Is your whole existence just going to church and remembering your own death?

I—read. Sometimes. And write. Poems? I don't read my own poetry, though. That would be conceited. No one else reads it either. I'm going to be a priest, eventually. Priests don't need to write poems.

Thou shalt not rhyme couplets?

The poems aren't good, Isaiah says. I wouldn't even get into the writing program at U of T. They only accept seven people a year.

Sounds like you've thought about it.

I'm not good. Enough. I'd embarrass myself.

Georgia raises her cigarette up like a glass.

To not being good.

Are you in school?

Fuck no, Georgia says. I thought about it. For acting. But I'd be stressed as fuck over all the work and broke from paying for rent in the city. I'd be miserable and alone.

You don't think you'd make friends?

My mom's my friend, Georgia says.

She's immediately aware of how stupid her remark sounds out loud.

Isaiah nods.

I understand, he says.

A pause.

Do you want to come back inside? he asks. We can sit together at the back where no one can see the vomit in your hair.

Georgia snorts.

Only if you don't try to convert me, she says.

The two of them sneak back inside. Isaiah dips his fingers in the baptismal font at the entrance. He places one hand on his stomach. He uses the other to touch his forehead. His chest. His left shoulder. His right shoulder.

They sit in the very back pew. Georgia watches Isaiah closely and copies his actions. She kneels when he kneels. Stands when he stands. Bows her head with him when Arlo speaks of breaking bread. The leaflet is a type of script, Georgia realizes. Another performance. Isaiah doesn't use a leaflet. His actions are muscle memory, permanently ingrained from years of practice.

A girl, maybe six or seven years old, belts each hymn from the pew behind them. She screams the words as if she's at a rock concert, her little voice hoarse and cracking.

Kit, her mother whispers harshly, you're embarrassing yourself.

When it is time to receive communion, Isaiah stands. Georgia watches him move up the line. Receive a wafer directly on his tongue. Grasp the gold chalice in both hands and take a sip of wine.

It is odd, Georgia realizes, to know the person responsible for your salvation outside of that context.

After the service, everyone folds their prayer benches back into place and collects their purses and their children. They file out of the church and congregate on the front steps, where Arlo is standing in his robes. The women gossip about how hot the inside of the church is and how their neighbours' lawns look unkempt and how they despise their daughters' boyfriends. They smoke and fan themselves with their leaflets. They blame the vomit out front on wild teenagers. The men laugh with Father Bloom about their city jobs and their cars that need new mufflers and their wives who don't have nearly enough sex with them. Georgia stands farther off with Isaiah until she sees her mother come out of the chapel, her blond hair frizzed from the humidity. Her brow furrows when she sees Georgia.

Where were you? Elsie asks. What is *on* you?

A hand appears on Elsie's shoulder. Arlo's.

I think the jokes in the sermon were too much, Arlo says. Tough crowd to crack.

They loved you, Elsie says. You're overthinking it.

Arlo turns his attention to Georgia.

Look at you, he says. All grown up.

The sentence is so natural, so innocent, almost as if it has been rehearsed.

It's nice to see you again, Father Bloom, she says.

Arlo, he says. Please. It's Arlo.

He turns back to Elsie.

The two of you must come to the vicarage for coffee.

Georgia opens her mouth to protest, but her mother is faster.

Absolutely, Elsie says.

I'll help with cleanup, Isaiah says quickly.

Georgia imagines a future twenty seconds from now in which she will have to stand alone with her mother and Arlo three feet away from her vomit and pretend that she is enjoying herself.

I'll, uh, help too, she says, following Isaiah back into the chapel before Elsie can say otherwise.

The chapel feels larger when it is empty. Wood creaks. An air conditioner hums. All the sounds seem to travel to the end of the aisle and back down again, from one wall to the other, near and far from each of Georgia's ears, like bouncing electrons.

Suddenly, she is alone. She hears shuffling to her left. A door opening and shutting. Isaiah talking to himself in the sacristy.

Georgia scans the rafters and counts the imperfections in the wood. One. Two.

Show yourself! She yells to the ceiling, confident that God will not answer, and that the silence will be proof He doesn't exist.

She brings her eyes back down. Looks down the aisle. Blinks.

The woman who was singing during service is kneeling at the altar.

Georgia can still hear Isaiah in the sacristy. She walks down the aisle, slowly, expecting her hallucination to disappear.

The dark-haired woman stays where she is. Perfectly still. She's changed out of her robes, kneeling in a black dress and black cardigan. Eyes shut. Hands clasped.

Georgia walks forward until she gets to the prayer railing. She attempts to copy the woman as quietly as she can, kneeling on the red-cushioned platform in front of her.

Georgia is convinced that prayer produces a placebo effect. That if she feels anything at all—which she is unlikely to—it will be self-manufactured calm or peace or emotion. When she shuts her eyes, she smells the woman's hair. The shampoo has a distinct, strong scent. Cheap and fruity like fake roses. She thinks about what the woman's shoulder-length bob must look like wet—dark and soaked with water, frothing suds, the scratch of fingernails massaging scalp.

She opens her eyes. Embarrassed. When she tries to stand back up, her elbow hits the railing. It rattles, the sound ringing through the space. The woman with the dark hair opens her eyes.

Sorry, Georgia says.

The woman smiles.

I forgive you.

Her face creases when she smiles—crow's feet and forehead lines. She seems older than Georgia, maybe in her late thirties.

Do you feel better afterwards? Georgia asks. After you come here?

Sometimes I feel worse, the woman says.

Georgia comes closer. Inspects the altar.

Why would you do something that makes you feel bad? she asks.

The woman shrugs. Her necklace sways—a bronze locket with a little blue bird.

Habit. You get comfortable.

Georgia looks at the kneeler. At the woman. At the altar.

Can I pray for you? the woman asks.

Sure, Georgia says, though she isn't sure at all.

The woman shuts her eyes.

My name's Georgia, by the way, Georgia adds. In case He, uh, needs my name.

I'm Felicity, the woman says.

Silence. Georgia waits.

Dear Lord, Felicity says, please protect Georgia throughout this day. Please help her to do the things that make her feel good, and the things that make her feel bad, and the things that don't make her feel anything at all—all of the things that make up a day in her life.

The woman opens her eyes. Looks at Georgia.

Amen, she says.

Georgia doesn't feel any different.

Thanks, she says. That wasn't too horrible.

It can be, Felicity says.

A pause.

Forgive me for that, she adds.

A slam down the aisle. Keys jangling. Footsteps. Isaiah's gait is awkward and clumsy like a fawn's. He turns to Felicity.

Ready to go, Mom?

She nods. Stands. Smooths her skirt.

I think we're all set, Felicity says.

Georgia forces a smile.

The vicarage isn't a quiet place. The house is too close to everything, Georgia thinks. The chapel. The road. The lake. When the church bells go off, they sound as if they're inside the vicarage itself. From the kitchen, Georgia can hear car horns and crosswalk alerts and day-drunk tourists singing.

The living room is filled with cardboard boxes not yet unpacked from the move. Mint-green wallpaper wraps around the room, but the walls are bare, framed paintings stacked in a corner. As far as Georgia can tell, hardcover books are the only thing that have been unpacked, stacked on the shelves of a large oak bookcase but not yet organized.

Elsie and Arlo sit together on an L-shaped couch. They keep their coffees on multicoloured coasters. Hardwood floors, scuffed from years of use. Arlo motions for his wife to join them, and Georgia watches as her demeanour transforms, like Arlo's did during the service. Her posture straightens, and she smiles at Elsie like a royal would smile at her subjects. With elegance. Poise. A little bit of pity. She keeps a hand on her husband's knee as Arlo and Elsie tell her stories from when they lived together. They laugh loudly and reference inside jokes that Felicity doesn't understand. She chuckles regardless. Her smile never slips—not even once. To be a priest's wife is to perform, and Felicity's stage directions are muscle memory.

Georgia sits at the kitchen table and eats extra-large marshmallows from a yellow plastic bag while Isaiah searches the boxes labelled *pantry* for hot chocolate mix. The room makes Georgia feel as though she is in a pioneer village house. Wooden spindle-backed chairs. Brown-and-orange tiled floor. Mustard-yellow cupboards. Chipped paint. Gas stove. A wooden centre island taking up far too much space. Lace curtains. Windows with the latches painted over, permanently shut.

The Blooms haven't gone grocery shopping since their arrival. The fridge is empty and takeout containers are stacked high in the recycling bin in the corner of the kitchen.

At one point, Isaiah thinks he's found the non-perishable food, but opens the box to find a stack of porcelain plates with years on them, wrapped in newspaper. One for each year Arlo and Felicity have been married. The first two plates were gifts from Felicity's father, Isaiah explains: one for Felicity and Arlo's wedding, and the other for their first anniversary. Isaiah's grandfather stopped sending them after that, but Arlo continued to order the annual plates from the same shop so that dinner guests would see how much The Blooms care about tradition.

Isaiah's bedroom is in the attic. It is the only room in the entire house that has been unpacked and organized and decorated. A wooden crucifix on the door and a laptop on the little wooden writing desk and a queen-sized bed with crisp white sheets where the ceiling slopes low overhead.

Georgia snoops through Isaiah's closet. She runs her hand through the cardigans.

Why do you own eleven of the same sweater?

They aren't the same, Isaiah says. They're different shades. This one is cream, and this one is beige.

Georgia wraps a blue striped tie around her neck. She knots it like a scarf. She begins to rummage through a pile of paperbacks on the closet floor.

Do you have a favourite book? Isaiah asks.

I don't read, Georgia lies.

You don't *read*? Anything?

Georgia shakes her head. She imagines Isaiah in her bedroom, with the book pages on the walls, and feels embarrassed. It is one of the many parts of Georgia that is ridiculous.

Isaiah throws his hands up in the air.

Okay, he says. Okay. I'm going to lend you a book. And then you can read it, and then we can discuss it.

You're giving me homework.

No, Isaiah says. This is what friends do. This is friendship.

Isaiah pushes all his hanging sweaters to one side of the closet. Stacks of notebooks and file folders and old childhood art projects covered in crayon. They are the only disorganized thing in the entire room.

He emerges with a book. Torn cover taped in place with Scotch tape. *Glass, Irony & God*, Anne Carson. He hands it to Georgia.

Who's James? she asks, looking at the inscription on the inside of the cover.

My mom's father, Isaiah says. This book was his.

The two of them go back downstairs. Arlo and Elsie and Felicity are still chatting and laughing. Elsie looks up at Georgia.

You keep disappearing today, she says.

There's still lots of today left, Georgia says. Better get me a leash.

Elsie rolls her eyes. She continues her conversation with Felicity. The two of them look odd together, Felicity in her black on black, thick nylons in shiny Mary Janes, Elsie in a white tank top and men's plaid button-down shirt and paint-covered jeans. Felicity sits with her hands in her lap, knees pushed tight together. Elsie sits cross-legged, crouched forward like she is looking closely at something. The taxidermist and the priest's wife. Georgia cannot imagine what they must be talking about. What they could have in common.

Isaiah joins the women on the couch. Arlo collects the coffee cups and brings them to the kitchen.

I forgot to offer you something to wear, Arlo says suddenly. You must want to clean up.

It takes a moment for Georgia to realize that Arlo is talking to her.

I do, Georgia says.

Arlo is suddenly beside her.

Felicity has a lot of clothes, he says. I'm sure something would fit you.

That would be nice, she says.

She glances back at her mother on the couch, absorbed in her conversation, before following Arlo down the hall to the master bedroom. More books—on the floor and the dresser and the desk. A bare mattress beside the deconstructed pieces of a bed frame. Clothes spilling out of garbage bags. Papers and tools and empty coffee cups.

Arlo pulls out a box from under the window.

Here we are, he says.

He rips the tape off the box with his teeth. Dumps its contents onto the floor.

Pick whatever you'd like, he says.

Georgia looks through the pile, feeling Arlo's eyes on her.

After some digging, Georgia finds a long-sleeved sage-green maternity dress with gold buttons down the back.

Can I take this? she asks.

Arlo nods, his eyes on her hands.

Absolutely, he says.

Georgia changes in the ensuite bathroom. She wets her hair in the sink and ties it back in a bun. Extra fabric in the middle of the dress droops over the place where a baby bump would be.

Arlo is folding laundry when Georgia walks back into the room. He smiles.

I'm glad it fits, he says. Do you want me to do up the buttons for you?

No, Georgia snaps. I'm fine.

Georgia reaches both of her arms behind her back, struggling to reach even a single button.

Fuck. Fucking fuck.

Arlo moves to help her, but she steps away. She reaches up and over her head, trying from a different angle.

You ran off, he says quietly.

What?

During service, Arlo continues. I saw you come in. But you didn't stay.

Georgia doesn't say anything. She is sweating. Breathing heavy. The dress stretches.

I hope it wasn't because of me, Arlo says.

It was, Georgia says.

She manages to take hold of a button. The button immediately falls out of its loop.

Arlo sighs. Moves towards Georgia again.

Georgia swats him away.

Are you going to tell my mom?

About what?

Georgia looks at him.

Would you like me to tell her? Arlo asks.

No.

Then we're on the same page.

Georgia pauses—realizes that locking the clasp at the very top of the dress will give it the illusion of being buttoned all the way up. She clicks it into place.

She turns to face Arlo.

Your wife is beautiful, she says. You're very lucky.

I am, Arlo says.

A pause.

Georgia.

Yes?

I'd like you to keep thinking about the arrangement I proposed last night. With my wife and me.

There's a heaviness in Georgia's stomach, now. An uncertainty. She has done this before: fallen in love with the idea of something without taking a moment to consider that maybe the idea of the thing was all she wanted. She once told a one-night stand that she *loved* when guys washed out her mouth with soap, even though she had never done it before. The boy-man obliged. He took her awkwardly by the hair and led her to the cracked porcelain sink in the hotel room bathroom and squeezed the entire contents of the travel-sized orchid-scented body wash onto her tongue because there weren't any of those prewrapped minibars of soap left. She vomited, and she sneezed bubbles for hours afterward, and they didn't have sex. She knew several seconds beforehand—just as the boy-man was unscrewing the cap of the body wash bottle—that she didn't want to go through with it. It wasn't too late to back out. She could've said that she'd changed her mind. But by then, she felt like she deserved to do something that she didn't want to do as a punishment for misunderstanding her own desires. She should've known earlier. She should've known all along.

What about my mom? she asks.

I would not think it wise to tell her, he says. Discretion would be key. That is, of course, if you're still interested.

If Elsie found out, it would be one more relationship of Elsie's that Georgia has ruined. She would never trust Georgia again. It would be Georgia's instigation, Georgia's secret-keeping, Georgia's betrayal, Georgia's fault.

The Blooms are not tourists. Georgia would have to face them every single day, and they would have to face the rest of Port Peter. How could she do that to Isaiah? Make him an outcast the moment he arrives? It's difficult enough to be twenty—he doesn't need the stress of being scarlet-lettered.

And yet, it is Arlo's desire for her—that feeling of being wanted, no matter what that wanting might lead to—that Georgia finds difficult to pass up. She will never be this young again, and she may never be wanted like this again. Being wanted is worth anything. Everything. And if the arrangement ends with anger and pain? Georgia can say, See? I told you. This is the kind of person I really am. The predictable boom and bust of a Port Peter summer turned to winter. Desire and its natural consequences.

The Blooms could be anyone. They could want anything. And Georgia would still come to the same decision.

I'm interested, she says.

Arlo smiles. He tucks a tuft of honey-blond hair behind Georgia's ear, his fingers lingering at her jaw.

That makes me very happy, he says. I value enthusiasm. And exclusivity.

You mean—not sleeping with anyone else? Just you and your wife?

Arlo nods.

Anything that might inspire you to up and leave Port Peter, he adds. It doesn't make sense for me to invest my time into something short-term or temporary.

I don't want to leave, Georgia says.

Good, Arlo says.

AUGUST 2008

Georgia has her first breakfast with Arlo and Felicity at six in the morning. It is the only time that Isaiah is out of the vicarage. He officiates matins and runs an early risers' Bible study for other young adults at St. Paul's from six until nine. This is where Georgia's mother thinks she is going when the two of them wake before dawn so that Elsie can open Buck Deco early for the tourists.

You waxed your legs and upper lip for—Jesus.

Look good, feel good, Mom, Georgia snaps. I'm trying to make a good impression.

Sounds like you already made a good impression on Isaiah.

It wasn't difficult for Georgia to convince her mother that Isaiah Bloom invited her to his Bible study out of the sweetness of his home-schooled, Anglo-Catholic heart, and that in exchange, Georgia agreed to show Isaiah around Port Peter later that afternoon. Though Georgia felt so guilty about lying that she offered to show Isaiah around Port Peter later that afternoon for real.

The sky is still tinged orange from sunrise when Georgia arrives at the vicarage. Arlo answers the door. He is in lay clothes—a navy pullover and black jeans—without a clergy collar. He smells like sea salt—his aftershave.

Felicity Bloom is dressed just as formally as when Georgia saw her last. A wool skirt, black, with a buttoned-up black cardigan. Opaque black footed tights. Fresh peachy blush on the apples of her cheeks. A perfume that smells expensive to Georgia—something with peonies and vanilla bean. Her dark brown bob is knife's-edge straight, tucked behind her ears. She has the same necklace on, the bronze chain and locket with the little blue bird, and she flutters around the kitchen with a nervous freneticism that makes Georgia feel like she's interrupting something important.

Flick, Arlo says. Look who's arrived.

Felicity turns and smiles at Georgia, but it isn't the same smile she had when the two of them were alone in St. Paul's, kneeling together. It is the same smile that a dog makes when you take your fingers and curl the edges of its mouth upward to make it look like it's smiling. It's funny when the dog smiles like a person, but you are aware that part of the joke is that you forced the dog to smile. Felicity's mouth smiles, but her eyes do not.

It's the first time Georgia considers the possibility that Arlo Bloom wants to bring another woman into his marital bed more than his wife does. Perhaps she took a lot of convincing. She is very pious, after all. Married a priest. Dresses conservatively. She made prayer look easy the first time she and Georgia met, as if she and God were intimate friends.

How would Georgia feel if she were in her late thirties and her husband brought home a twenty-one-year-old woman? She would absolutely compare herself to her counterpart. To be in your early twenties is to think that you are invincible. Glowing with an idea disguised as a fact: you will never be desired as much as you are in this moment.

Felicity Bloom explains that her plan was to make French

toast with fresh raspberries, sprinkled with icing sugar, but the farmers' market downtown only had peaches—which give Felicity hives—and she couldn't find the box labelled *kitchen* that held the frying pans, whisks, and spatulas. She assembles bowls of Raisin Bran cereal and soy milk for herself, her husband, and Georgia. They only have two clean dinner spoons, so Georgia eats her cereal with a massive serving spoon.

Should I put on some music? Arlo asks between bites.

I'm good, Georgia says.

She uses the giant spoon to take out each individual raisin and put it on the Virgin Mary napkin at her place setting.

You are good as in you are fine without music, Arlo asks, or you are good as in you are fine *with* music?

Whatever, Georgia says, shrugging.

The bran is soggy. Like eating wet chicken feed from an egg farm. Like Georgia is being fattened up to be loaded into a McDonald's truck. I would make a particularly good chicken nugget, she thinks. I would be the best nugget: crispy and tender and fucking delicious.

Our bedroom is down the hall, Arlo says finally.

Right, Georgia says.

No one moves.

Should we—go there? Georgia asks.

Felicity nods.

Arlo nods.

Georgia nods.

No one moves.

If you've changed your mind, Arlo says, I completely understand.

Nope, Georgia says. No, I'm—all ready. To go.

Silence.

Georgia stands because she knows that if she doesn't, no one will, and the three of them will be sitting at the table in front of their Raisin Bran for all eternity.

The Blooms still haven't unpacked their bedroom. Georgia has to step over a garbage bag of clothes to get to the centre of the room, where there is ample space for the three of them to stand. She eyes the framed Madonna and child above the bed.

Should we, like, cover them?

Felicity is already undressing. Unbuttoning her black cardigan, unzipping her black skirt. Peeling off her stockings. Arlo does not touch his clothes. He stands rigid, wringing his hands.

No? Georgia asks. Cool. I'm sure the Lord has seen, you know. All of it. Before.

Felicity is down to her bra and underwear. She looks at Arlo, eyes narrow.

Waiting for the rapture? she asks.

Arlo mutters something to himself, his brow furrowed. He unbuckles his belt.

Georgia takes off her jean jacket, under the impression that stripping is what's happening now. Georgia is positive that all parties, including herself, are bone-dry. Is this how all married people have sex? Is it always like eating unseasoned chicken breast?

The moment is even odder once they are all naked. Not only is Georgia's costume gone, but so is everyone's. They are rolls and patches of dry skin and stretch marks and scars and tufts of hair. They are asymmetrical breasts and wide feet. Jutting ribs. Ass dimples. Georgia is just—a person. And the Blooms are just people.

What would you like us to do? Arlo asks his wife.

Felicity smiles. For real. She turns to Georgia.

I'd like you to hit him.

Georgia doesn't move.

Did you say—hit him?

Yes, Felicity says. Just don't knock his teeth out.

Georgia looks to Arlo for confirmation that Felicity is, in fact, joking. But his answer proves otherwise.

You heard the woman, he says.

Georgia considers herself to be decent at reading people. When she first met Arlo, the two of them smoking outside the convenience store, she was certain she knew what he would be like in bed. It was obvious. He takes the lead in every conversation and interaction. He is confident. She anticipated a situation in which she would, very happily, not need to make a single decision because all the decisions would be made for her. He would tie her up. Carry her around. Maybe fuck her over the bathroom sink. He would grip her tight and position her how he saw fit and she would be a water fountain of a woman. It is a fantasy that makes perfect sense if not thought about for too long, as all fantasies do.

Plenty of men have hit Georgia. About half of them hit her because she asked them to. She has never allowed herself to imagine what it might feel like to be the one with the power.

Georgia slaps Arlo's face with her open palm. He doesn't flinch, but instead lets the momentum of the blow turn his head to one side. She winces at the sound, pulling her hand away. She leaves a faint red mark on Arlo's cheek. For a moment, Georgia thinks that he might hit her back.

Instead, he chuckles.

I think you can hit me harder than that, Georgia, he says.

She does, and it is harder and louder than either of them

expects. The momentum makes him sway. He blinks, bringing his hand up to his face, feeling the heat.

Georgia's hand stings, but a kind of electricity hums through her body. From her eyelids to her toes. Again. She would like to hit him again.

Kiss him, Felicity says.

Georgia turns and realizes that Felicity is no longer standing beside her, but is lying in her and Arlo's bed, atop the duvet. Her eyes are focused, as if Arlo and Georgia are competing in a contest and Felicity is the judge.

Georgia takes Arlo's face in both hands and kisses hard, with tongue. She understands now what this is. An audition. A performance. She sucks his bottom lip, grazing it with her teeth. Arlo holds the back of her head with one hand and the small of her back with the other. He pulls her tight against his body.

When Georgia breaks away from Arlo, Felicity is cradling her head in her hand. She yawns.

Georgia turns back to Arlo.

Could you, um, get on the ground? she asks him.

Is that a question?

Another glance at Felicity. Back to Arlo.

No, Georgia says. You should—lie down. On the floor.

Surprisingly, Arlo does what he is told.

Georgia blocks her movements in her head. She has been cast in a show with an audience of one, and that audience wants to leave satisfied.

A Liturgy For Pleasure

The Leader (Georgia) sits on the Husband's face. His mouth is full of her. The Leader bucks back and forth like she is on a bull ride.

The Leader: (thinking about what she will make to eat when she gets home) You like that?

All present moan.

*The Wife touches herself. She rubs in slow, clockwise circles. She remembers that the bread in the cupboard has moulded. Glances at **the Leader**, tries to ignore the sublime in the peaks and valleys of **the Leader**'s body, ignores the way **the Leader**'s hair sticks to her forehead with sweat, ignores her mouth, open, swearing, gasping, devouring the world. She tries to make a mental list of what other groceries the Blooms need. Jam. Butter. Fuck. Onions. Fucking hell. Coffee beans.*

The Husband: [inaudible]

*The Leader bends forward, her stomach on **the Husband**'s chest. She takes him in her mouth. Stopping halfway. Flicking her tongue back and forth over the tip. Drool drips. The spittle before a rainstorm.*

*The Husband curls his tongue in response. He laps **the Leader** up. He spells out entire hymns inside her.*

Georgia slides forward and spins herself around so that she is facing Arlo while she straddles him. The two of them look at each other, hungry, panting.

What now? Arlo asks Felicity.

Felicity's eyes widen. She hesitates.

Please, she mutters.

No, Arlo snaps. You tell me what you want.

Felicity looks as though she might cry. Her arms are crossed.

Arlo sighs.

You *asked* me to ask her, he says. You wanted this.

Then what are you waiting for?

I'm not going to fail another fucking test, Flick, Arlo snaps. If you don't want this, you need to say so. Right now.

I'm not a kid.

Stop acting like one then.

Arlo grips Georgia's hips and slowly guides her down onto him, while Georgia looks at Felicity, trying to figure out what exactly is going on, what exactly Felicity wants out of this.

It isn't perfect, not exactly the right spot, not the very specific thing that she needs in that moment, but it is enough. She shifts to get comfortable, and the friction sub- sides—little by little—and the work begins, her abs tight, her thighs flexed, jolts of sensation each time she rises and falls, and Arlo's eyes are shut, his mouth agape, his fingers digging into her sides, and Georgia looks back at Felicity— this woman who is the universe—still keeping her rhythm, hoping to find something in Felicity's dark eyes that affirms she is doing a good job—something that sees her not as a body, but as a person—and Felicity's eyes are shut, and she is touching herself again, quickly now, and Georgia can't think of anything to say—her voice caught—and she tries to remember who it is in the Bible who had a stutter, and she can't recall, and she thinks that maybe, if you can't say something the way you want to, it is better not to say any- thing at all, and Arlo bucks—fucking her harder now—and Georgia's eyes are still on Felicity, and Georgia imagines that it is just the two of them—years from now—in a city apartment somewhere loud, and busy, with artisan markets, and burger shops, open late, and it is Felicity and Georgia who are married—it is Felicity, and Georgia, who are, one flesh, and Felicity, touches, Georgia, and after, they make love, the two, of them, will lie, together and talk, about the trip, to Paris, they would like, to take, next year, and they, will think, about the new, fresh, giddy, kind of, love they both had, when they, first met, and then, Felicity will make, Georgia bread, or they will, make it, together, their careful, fingers braiding, the dough, with grace, and Felicity, will dot, flour on, Georgia's nose, and Georgia, will sneeze, and Felicity, will say, God, bless, you, and, take Georgia's, face, in, her, hands, and, tell, her, I, love, you, I, love, you, her, lips, her, hands, her, hair, her, breath, nose, neck, ears, nails, God, is, a, She, and, She, is, right, here, Flick—, Flick—, Flick—, Flick—

And Arlo is finished.

He slides her off him, leaves the room, and returns with a wet washcloth to clean her. Felicity is no longer touching herself, but her gaze is still on Georgia, both their faces flushed bright red.

Then Arlo retreats to the bathroom without a word, and Felicity and Georgia are alone.

When Georgia opens her mouth, her brain overlaps Was that what you wanted? and Was I okay?

Was I what you wanted? she ends up asking.

Felicity nods. Realizes what she is nodding to. Stops. Her palms on her cheeks. Shakes her head. Stops again.

Georgia stammers, I meant something else. I mean, not that. Not what I just said—

Thank you, Felicity interrupts.

You too, Georgia says.

Arlo returns fully dressed.

I'll drive you home when you're ready.

In the car, Georgia is still breathless. The sun is just beginning to reach its full height and heat and brightness of the day. Arlo keeps a hand on her knee as he drives, as if to say, Don't leave. Where would she go?

She almost forgets who she is with. Where she is coming from. Until Arlo speaks.

What was your favourite part? he asks, his eyes still on the road.

Georgia doesn't know what to say. Her mind wheels through a foggy future. Love. Paris. Bread. Flour.

All of it, Georgia says.

They are on Georgia's street now, her house coming into view.

Would you like to do it again? Arlo asks.

How many people could her decision affect? Georgia. Arlo. Felicity. Elsie. Isaiah. Elsie. Isaiah. Felicity. Isaiah. Elsie. Isaiah. Felicity. Felicity. Felicity. Felicity.

Yes, Georgia says.

Elsie and Georgia drink boxed wine in coffee mugs on Elsie's double bed and watch a documentary about Jon-Benét Ramsey. She was murdered twelve years ago, but CBC's *The Fifth Estate* airs the interviews with her family for the tenth anniversary at least three times a month. Dried butterflies sit in frames above Elsie's TV, their wings pinned to reveal all their colours. Georgia turns up the volume. JonBenét's brother laughs and talks about her funeral.

The dad did it, Elsie says. I mean, obviously. He was abusing her and wanted to cover it up.

Do you think the mom knew? Georgia asks.

Elsie nods.

It's in a mom's DNA to know if something like that is happening to their kid. It's an instinct, like a—you know. You know what I mean.

A sixth sense, Georgia says.

Exactly. Moms always know.

Georgia doesn't say anything. She downs the rest of her wine in a single gulp. Then she cuddles in close, leaning her head on Elsie's shoulder.

AUGUST 2008

Isaiah knows he is being watched. The cashier at the drugstore. The older man with the ice cream cart selling treats on the beach. The woman behind Isaiah at the bank, so close she accidentally steps on the backs of his heels. Even a few of the congregants at St. Paul's—a handful of locals in a sea of tourists coming to a destination church to absolve themselves of their holiday sins—look at Isaiah Bloom as if he has done something wrong.

Isaiah was essentially invisible in Minden. It was obvious that his father wasn't exactly gentle. There were bruises. Moments at the Advent Bazaar or the summer parish picnic when Arlo lost his patience and was less than subtle about his reprimand. Opportunity after opportunity for someone—anyone—to say something. To ask Isaiah if he was okay. And no one did. It didn't matter that Isaiah had grown up with these people, that he saw them four days a week for almost twenty years, because when he needed them most, they valued their comfort over his safety. People think that being a part of something is the same thing as having support, but it isn't, Isaiah thinks. One good person is support; a group of people is an audience.

But in Port Peter, Isaiah is seen even when he doesn't want to be. He apologizes for existing at Bible study and at the baby clothes store and at the bakery that only sells peach muffins and iced coffee with Red Bull. *Sorry* leaves his lips so often that it doesn't even sound like a real word anymore. He buys something at every boardwalk shop he enters so that people don't think he's stealing: a braided bracelet and a pineapple milkshake and a key chain shaped like a peach. He grips the wad of receipts in his fist so tight that they soften. He is embarrassed by his paranoia.

By the time he gets to the end of the boardwalk, his white wool sweater is soaked with sweat, and there is sand in his leather dress shoes. His dark curls frizz up in the lakeside humidity. Isaiah knows it gets hot down here by this point in the summer. Still, he doesn't want to accidentally be underdressed.

Georgia's text message instructs Isaiah to meet her at the purple dessert shop at the end of the boardwalk at twelve o'clock sharp. From afar, the building looks like a public washroom. He doesn't see the colour until he is much closer. Its brick is painted plum. Gold trim accents every edge of every window and corner. Even the eavestroughs sparkle. The shop's only outside identification is a hand-painted sign on the teal door:

CRIME BRÛLÉE DESSERTS
OPEN WHEN IN NEED

He pulls the handle but the door is locked. He gets up on his tiptoes and attempts to look through the peephole.

The door opens, knocking him back, and there is Georgia Jackson, her blond hair tucked behind her ears, wearing a baby-blue Victorian-style nightgown as a crop top, tied in a knot above her belly button, and a long white circle skirt that covers her feet.

The linoleum floor inside has been painted black, and the ceiling is a lush crimson. Every inch of the inside wall is covered in yellowed newspaper. Little metal patio tables, also painted black, line the space, and the accompanying metal chairs are wrapped in yellow caution tape tied off with a bow at the back. Isaiah rests his hand against the wall and reads the first sentence his eyes fall upon: *Leonard Jennings is survived by his four grandchildren*. He glances at another page above. Then another. The walls are covered in obituaries.

An older woman stands behind the counter in a green tube top. She waves at him. Smile lines decorate her face.

See, Lee? Georgia says, pointing to Isaiah. I have living, breathing friends.

Lee leans forward and squints at Isaiah. She shakes her finger.

Isaiah Bloom, she says.

Georgia raises an eyebrow.

You know him?

No, Lee says. But you look like my old neighbour. Isaiah Peter Bloom.

It takes Isaiah a moment to grasp what is happening.

Oh, he says finally. You mean my granddad. My dad's dad. We have the same name.

Lee nods. Slowly.

Your father is Arlo, then? One of the twins?

Yes, Isaiah says. The living one.

Silence.

Do you, um, have hot chocolate here? Isaiah asks, changing the subject. I don't drink coffee. Just hot chocolate. Sorry.

I can make you hot chocolate, Lee says. You want food?

Isaiah nods. Says nothing. Lee waits for him to order, but he just stands there, smiling and nodding. She sighs.

I'll just surprise you then, she says, straight-faced.

She disappears into the kitchen.

Georgia leads Isaiah to one of the caution tape–wrapped tables. Slides into her seat.

Do you like that you're named after your grandfather? she asks.

Isaiah shrugs. He never met his father's father while he was still alive. Since arriving in Port Peter, Arlo has often brought up his father when he and Isaiah are on their own, driving through town. Arlo seems to live in a limbo between memory and reality, unable to see landmarks or stores or any downtown locations without a layer of his childhood and adolescence over top. To Arlo, past events are like tracing paper: he can see the present version of each place in town if he focuses hard enough, tracing the outline to complete a picture, but it will always be a copy of what it once was. The boardwalk will never be a mere boardwalk—it will forever be the place from which a six-year-old Arlo dropped his mitten on the ice of frozen Lake Ligeia, and from which his father pushed him forward to retrieve it. Where he fell through the ice and struggled to find the opening as his body began to shut down from the pain and the cold. Where his father pulled him up and said the only reason he did so was because he didn't have the money to pay for a fucking funeral.

After lunch, Georgia takes Isaiah through the heart of Port Peter. She shows him the green electrical box behind Peter Isobar Public School where she was dared to kiss the weird shortstop from intramural soccer baseball. She shows him the funeral home on Elizabeth Street that used to be a Jumbo Video.

You can tell, she says, pointing to the window frames. The paint hasn't changed. It's the same blue.

She finds two dimes on the ground and takes him for a ride on the carousel. The carousel near the beach was here when Isaiah's father was little. It hasn't changed its ticket price since then. It might break down at any moment. It plays loud circus music as it spins. Georgia picks a lion standing on its hind legs. It goes up and down. Isaiah picks a powder-blue bench.

She shows him the park by the beach, with the rusted chain-link fence and the playground shaped like a massive pirate ship coming up out of the ground. They fill their pockets with beach glass and smooth stones and cratered rocks like little moons.

She shows him Spot Street, a dead-end road off the beach parking lot where people leave their unwanted kittens after scraggly strays knock up their shiny black house cats. The two of them fill their hands with cat food and let teary-eyed felines eat right out of their palms like goats at a petting zoo.

I named them all after kitchen items when they were just babies, Georgia says. The white one with the pink nose is Spatula. That skinny tabby is Ladle. One of those orange ones is Fridge—I think it's the one with a nub for a tail.

Isaiah buys a black sun hat at one of the tourist shops on the boardwalk. He carries it around with him at first, but eventually he feels brave enough to put it on. There is no one here to tell him that he looks foolish. No one here to take it from him. He and Georgia sit in the sand and split a BeaverTail covered in peanut butter and Skittles.

Georgia leads Isaiah down a forest path as the sun is setting. The sky melts hot drips of orange and red. Sailor's delight, Isaiah thinks.

The path opens onto a patch of beach, directly underneath the cliffside lookout. They walk until they reach a slice of cliff that juts far forward into the lake, cutting the beach to a dead end. Most people don't bother trying to get around it. Those who do try must have three qualities:

• They are not afraid of swimming in an undertow.

• They are not afraid of thick algae and what lives within it.

• They are not afraid of the possibility of being unable to return the way they came.

Georgia removes her green rubber boots and places them in the sand.

We'll have to wade through the water a bit, she says. There's something on the other side that I want to show you.

Isaiah hesitates. He looks down at his dress shoes. His knitted sweater.

Okay, he says.

He slips his shoes off, then peels off his socks, folding them neatly and tucking them inside the shoes. He follows Georgia into Lake Ligeia almost fully clothed.

The green water is warmer in some places and cooler in others. Georgia wades up to her armpits before swimming around the rock face. Isaiah trips on what he thinks is a rock, but is really a sleeping snapping turtle, and falls into the water face first. He expects to taste algae, but tastes something else instead. Copper.

Isaiah sees the top of a lighthouse in the distance as soon as he rounds the rock face. Instead of a beach, there are hundreds of massive boulders piled against the cliffside.

They climb the rocks in their bare feet, as if walking on all fours, until the beach returns. Isaiah follows Georgia along the shore for another five minutes. The cliffside opens its mouth in an overhang. It takes Isaiah a moment to realize that it is a cave.

The cave smiles wide with stalactite teeth. It is the kind of smile that people only give when they have a secret that will ruin your life. The rock walls drip with water. Georgia only walks a foot into the cave before turning back towards the water and sitting down.

See? Sublime sunset viewing, she says.

Isaiah turns. The sun is a deep red, and the sky is an explosion of fire, layer after layer of different orange shades, making the green water shimmer below. Isaiah wants to remember this image forever. He sits on the cave floor beside Georgia.

What's that? he asks, pointing to the outline of what looks like a pirate ship, shadowed against the horizon.

The Grande Arabella, Georgia says. It crashed here in, like, eighteen-whatever. They turned it into a floating restaurant for the tourists, but no one who actually lives here can afford to eat there.

How do you even get on?

They have staff who row you. It's a whole fucking experience.

She wiggles her toes. The two of them begin to ask each other questions.

If you could change one thing about my life, what would you change? Georgia asks.

I would dye your hair pink, Isaiah says. To match your personality. But only the wash-out stuff in case you didn't like it. Do you believe in soulmates?

Yes, Georgia says. I think so. What do you lie about most often?

How I'm feeling, Isaiah says. Like, if I'm feeling bad, I'll say I'm feeling good. You know.

I know.

What do you lie to *yourself* about most often? he asks.

That I'm doing the right thing, Georgia says, when I'm really doing something bad. What do you want more than anything else in the world?

A pause.

I don't think about those kinds of things very often.

Georgia waits.

My own apartment, he says finally. With tall bookshelves.

His mind wanders further.

I would have tea in the cupboards. And hot chocolate. Lots of different kinds of drinks. And mugs from the thrift store. And a pet budgie. A yellow one.

You could buy tea now, Georgia suggests. You don't need your own apartment for that.

Isaiah pauses.

Yeah, he says quietly. I could do that.

I almost auditioned for acting school in the city, Georgia says. I wrote a monologue and everything.

Almost?

I chickened out. I didn't want to leave my mom here by herself.

Do you still have the monologue?

I memorized it.

I would like to hear it.

No, you wouldn't.

I would.

What, now?

Yes.

Georgia scowls.

You don't have to, Isaiah says.

Let me find it.

Isaiah waits.

Okay, Georgia says. Okay. So, I'm this girl, a teenager, and she's trying to write a suicide note, right? She's upset and she's decided that this is it. There was this *incident*, bad shit leading up to it, but this time was the very worst. It was so bad that it had to be the last thing to ever happen to her. So she's, like, leaving a letter for her mother, but she can't get it exactly right. It's very difficult to find the right words, but she's trying. Okay. Here we go.

Georgia clears her throat.

Dear Mom, she says. I'm sorry that I'm a bad day, and that I'm a shitty moment, and a difficult week, and a hard life. I'm sorry that I'm so hard to love. This is hard to write. Everything is hard. No. Sorry. I'll start over.

Dear Mom, I am bad. No. Start over.

Dear Mom, I wish I could be better. I wish there was a better, and that I knew what it looked and smelled like, and I wish I could hold the picture of it in my head, and I wish I could imagine an existence where you and I were better than we are right now, where we aren't fighting, and I wish you would believe me about what he did while you were at work. While you were working. While we were watching movies. While we watched movies. While the movies were on. Wait. Start over.

Dear Mom, the smell of popcorn makes me nauseous. I can still smell him even though he is gone. He is gone. I'm sorry. Start over.

Dear Mom, I lied about getting my period at fourteen. I didn't actually get it until two years later. Everyone else at school was getting it and I felt left out. And then you were so proud, and you went and bought me that gold-filled necklace, the one that says *Mother & Daughter* on it. Because before it was you, a woman, and me, a girl, and then finally it was two women, side by side, taking on the world together. Start over.

Dear Mom, I don't want to die. How can you want something that you know nothing about? Start over.

Mom, I'm sorry.

Georgia stops. Looks up.

Thank you for sharing that, Isaiah says. I liked it a lot.

Really?

Yes.

I guess it doesn't matter now, though, she says.

I think that it does, Isaiah says.

He shivers. The evening brings cold. An owl bellows from a tree nearby, calling her children home to bed.

SEPTEMBER 1970

The sky below Lake Ligeia is sickly green and brown. It is always dark, but the grass is lush and wild and filled with blue forget-me-nots. The grass is also littered with dry bones. Knuckles. Teeth. Little skulls, half buried in the dirt. Every meal is a picnic without a blanket. It is a large, relaxed, communal affair.

One of the Birds leaves early in the morning and returns with food. Loaves of French bread and wheels of soft cheese. Red grapes and moist dates and plump plums and tangerines. Bottles of Niagara Peninsula red wine. Baskets and baskets of peaches.

Hills roll on in the distance, but most of the Birds have never explored them. They come up out of the water onto the Port Peter cliffside and stay for the day. When it is time to return home after a day of sleeping and drinking, they retreat to the meadow beneath the lake.

The Birds sleep in massive sunken ships, broken apart in the meadow. Each ship has a cabin. The boats have tattered sails and splintered decks and haven't touched water for hundreds of years. A long time ago, they were in the lake; now, they are here, turned on their sides, full of Birds.

Four weeks after meeting James, Kind is seasick from her morning swim in the lake. She vomits in the meadow flowers while the other Birds hunt. She is almost too tired to hold herself up. The vomit gets in her long hair. Lila stands behind her. She frowns.

What? Kind asks.

I was like this, too, Lila says. That boy you weren't supposed to talk to—he put a baby in you.

It takes Kind a moment to absorb what Lila has said. And she feels a wetness from her eyes. Down her cheeks. Not of fear, but of joy.

THE SECOND PART OF BIRD SUIT

CALLED

RIPEN

JUNE 1996

The best Port Peter peaches are grown on Kind Farms off Highway 24. The orchards have been there since before Georgia was born. Other farms came first—Smith Orchards and the Willabee Family Farm—but Kind Farms was the first to let visitors pick their own peaches. The orchards used to belong to a man named Bill Rickles, who didn't know how to take care of peach trees. He let them overgrow during some seasons and butchered good branches during others. The peaches came out more yellow than gold, with too much fuzz, and he ripped them off the trees when they were only the size of tennis balls. He tried to sell his below-average peaches at the summer farmers' market in town, but not even the fruit flies wanted a bite. He'd haul them back home and try to preserve them as canned jams, but he never got the hang of sealing the lids airtight, and the jams always moulded in their glass jars. His cellar shelves were stacked with his accidental experiments.

One summer, when Elsie Jackson was a teenager, Bill managed to sell his land to a younger woman from a nearby town. She bought the orchards and his house on the property for an incredible lump sum. No one knows quite how much. It was enough for Bill to move to Tahiti, or Venice, or somewhere else far away and beautiful, because no one in town saw Bill after that.

The people of Port Peter noticed a change by the next spring. The trees were taller and lusher, the soil better taken care of. The peaches were golden and juicy and grew larger and larger every year. Instead of a few cratefuls, Kind Farms had so many peaches each summer that they started shipping them out of the country on transport trucks and selling them in grocery stores across the globe.

No one has met the original buyer. She runs Kind Farms remotely, in constant contact with the farmhands and storefront managers, all of whom are women, and none of whom are locals. Only they know where she is. During tourist season, the women organize peach picking and tractor rides. Tourists can buy peach jam, peach butter, and other artisanal preservatives from the storefront run out of Bill's old house. The women are always singing—in the store and in the orchard and at the farm gates as they greet visitors. Their voices are almost sweeter than the peaches.

Georgia remembers a trip to Kind Farms she went on when she was ten, with her mother and her mother's boyfriend Joshua-Jonathan.

I'm sick of peaches, she whined from the back seat of her mother's Corolla. And it's too hot. My stomach hurts.

Keep complaining and you'll know what real hurt feels like, Joshua-Jonathan snapped.

He took Elsie on a romantic tractor ride for grown-ups and told Georgia to entertain herself. She took off her rubber boots and socks and left them in the parking lot. She walked around the orchard in her bare feet, feeling the cold grass between her toes. Each walkway was walled by rows of peach trees less than ten feet tall. They were thick and round, with some branches so low to the ground that they looked more like giant bushes than they did trees. Fist-sized peaches pulled the branches down. Some peaches hung at eye level, and others touched the grass path, and others rolled around in the dirt at the base of the trunks. Kids younger than Georgia sprinted past her, pitching the peaches like snowballs.

Georgia walked until her arms were sunburnt light red and her toenails were packed with dirt. She walked until the crowd of peach-picking tourists thinned into a smattering of solo orchard enthusiasts here and there, and she kept going until she was completely alone in a section of the orchard so far from the storefront that the voices of others sounded more like echoes. What if she just stayed lost? Who would care? Not Joshua-Jonathan, certainly. Maybe her mother, but she and her boyfriend could have another baby, one that belonged to them both, and the memory of Georgia could fade from Elsie's mind with ease.

Do you want to play with us? a small voice asked.

Georgia turned. Three girls stood behind her on the path. One looked to be about Georgia's age, with long black curls down to her hips. The second was taller, but appeared younger, with a bright ginger chin-length bob. The third girl couldn't have been older than five, with warm-brown braids hanging over both shoulders. All three girls wore matching baby-blue cotton T-shirts and white cut-off overalls. None of them wore shoes, but unlike Georgia, their toes were perfectly clean.

What are you playing? Georgia asked.

Captain Peter and the Birds, the girl with brown braids said. We're pretending it's the last night on the Grande Arabella. The night his crew jumped overboard.

I like pretending, Georgia said.

The four of them climbed the trees and hung off the branches as if they were swinging on metal monkey bars.

Georgia played the part of Captain Peter.

Your loyalty means everything to me! she shouted to her crew. Who will I be if you leave me? A captain without a crew is just some guy! A guy who everyone abandons!

The other girls giggled. They tugged on Georgia's ankles until she fell on top of them in the grass, and then they were a whole pile of laughter, covered in earth. They ate the big, fresh peaches that had fallen on the ground, still smudged with soil, and got sweet nectar and dark dirt on their lips and chins and teeth. They unbraided and rebraided one another's hair with sticky hands. They napped under the shade of the peach tree branches.

When Georgia finally woke, the hot sun had hidden behind a group of clouds. The three girls stood over her.

Why didn't you wake me? Georgia asked.

We tried, the black-haired one said. We thought you might be dead. We sang to you.

I didn't hear any singing, Georgia said.

The three girls exchanged glances.

We need to go back home now, before it gets too late, the smallest one said.

Can I go with you? Georgia asked. We can play more of our game.

The girl with the braids smiled.

Not tonight, she said. But soon. Maybe.

How will I find you?

Listen for singing while you're in bed at night, she said. Follow the singing right out your front door. If it gets louder, you'll be going the right way. Like the game Marco Polo.

Like Marco Polo, Georgia repeated.

And she waited awake in her twin bed, her window cracked open in anticipation. She heard crickets in the rose

bushes outside, and drunk tourists smashing glass beer bottles along John Street, and Joshua-Jonathan yelling at her
mother on the front porch, but she didn't hear any singing.
Not that night. Not any night.

JANUARY 2004

When Isaiah is fourteen, Arlo brings him to visit his mother's father. To Isaiah's surprise, he doesn't live in Boston, but just across town. Arlo Bloom has not spoken to his father-in-law since his and Felicity's wedding. By extension, Felicity has not been permitted to see her father. This instance in January is the first and last time Isaiah meets his grandfather.

The Victorian house sits at the top of an uphill street on the edge of Minden. Four stories. Massive windows with Juliet balconies. Back courtyard. Overgrown weeds and wildflowers cover the walking path up to a dark arched wooden door with a stained glass window. Ivy covers the house like hair growing from a head, curling in every direction, but controlled as if part of the structure itself.

Isaiah drowns in his father's black suit jacket. His lanky limbs wear the formal clothes as if they were elaborate curtains and his body simply the rod. Arlo fidgets with the clergy collar poking out from beneath his double-breasted peacoat once every minute or so. He knocks on the front door—twelve loud raps in quick succession. Silence. He and Isaiah wait in the cold.

They are about to give up when Isaiah's grandfather opens the door. He is younger than Isaiah expects, perhaps in his midsixties. A head of silver hair. Summer sky–blue eyes. Crooked nose.

Arlo stands straight and stiff. Isaiah has never seen his father so nervous.

James, Arlo says.

The man says nothing. His eyes narrow at Arlo, seeing him in a way that most people hope they are never seen.

For a moment, it seems to Isaiah that his grandfather will not let him and his father inside. That they came here for nothing.

Then, James looks over at Isaiah. At his dark curls. His deep brown eyes.

Come in, then, James mutters. You'll get frostbite.

Arlo exhales audibly.

As they walk down the main hallway, Arlo taps his son on the shoulder and points to a dark room on their left.

Your grandfather and I have something to discuss, he says. You can wait in there.

Isaiah goes where he is directed. The room is a library. Tall redwood shelves stretch upward just short of the high ceiling, built right into the walls themselves. The shelves have gaps where art sits. A ship in a bottle. A jade vase. A massive oil painting of an elderly man and a young boy wearing matching yellow rain boots. From across the room, the painting looks so lifelike that Isaiah is convinced it is a photograph. When he walks closer, he sees the texture of the paint on the canvas, each individual brush stroke, cracked in some places and peaked in others, almost rubbery. The piece's imperfections are now in full view. Isaiah thinks of his father, who is often close enough to those around him to be admired but distant enough that they will never see the parts of him that make him something mortal. Something real.

Isaiah inspects the books at eye level on the shelf closest to him. He runs his hand along the spines. The books are all worn paperbacks, rather than the hardcovers he expects.

Isaiah walks back towards the arched entrance to the library and pokes his head into the hallway. He can see his father and grandfather in the kitchen at the end of the hall. Arlo is pacing back and forth, talking with his hands. James sits in a kitchen chair. He is silent while Arlo's voice gets louder and louder.

Isaiah goes back into the library. He listens carefully to ensure that no one is walking back down the hallway. Then he slowly pulls a book with a black spine from one of the shelves.

He looks at the doorway again before flipping the book over. It is black with white text. Isaiah cannot tell if the painting on the cover is abstract, or if he is too dumb to figure out what it is supposed to be. The background is brown and patchy like dirt thrown all over a white floor, and there are faint pencil drawings of lines and leaves and odd shapes. The foreground is thick red and black with bright yellow strokes. It is a cacophony of textured oil paint—two black peaks, perhaps volcanoes, spewing fireballs or fingerprints. The painting is cut off two-thirds up the cover. The title sits, isolated, on nothing but a plain black background.

Glass, Irony & God
Anne Carson

For a moment, he considers putting the book back in its place without opening it. He hasn't done anything wrong *yet*, after all.

Another glance at the doorway. Isaiah exhales. He opens the book to a random page.

And he blinks, convinced that he cannot possibly be reading the words correctly. Sure enough, there they are, exactly as he saw them the first time. *Book of Isaiah.*

Shouting down the hallway. A voice—Arlo's. James's over top. They interrupt one another, getting louder and louder.

Suddenly, Isaiah hears footsteps down the hallway. Without thinking, he shoves the book in his jacket's inside pocket.

Arlo walks into the library. His face is flushed.

We're leaving, he says.

Isaiah nods. He can feel the book poking into his ribs. He follows his father to the entryway. Arlo opens the door before Isaiah can even tie the first of his brown leather boots. It is snowing. The cold air nips at his eyes and cheeks. It is a painful sensation. Suddenly, James is standing over him, his arms crossed.

Your mother can't stay here, son, he says to Isaiah. She needs to go home.

Isaiah furrows his eyebrows.

She is home, he says. She's sleeping in her bed right now.

Isaiah can feel his father's eyes on him from the doorway, and when he finally looks up, he is surprised to find Arlo's grey-blue eyes tinged red, welling with tears.

Isaiah, Arlo says, his voice cracking. Please. Let's go.

Isaiah ties off his second boot and stands. The book in his pocket shifts slightly, but thankfully doesn't fall out. Arlo grips Isaiah's shoulders from behind and leads him out the door. The two of them are halfway down the driveway when James calls out.

You kill everyone around you, he says.

Isaiah's grandfather is still standing in the doorway when Isaiah and Arlo pull out of the driveway. Isaiah watches James's body get smaller and smaller as they drive away, until it becomes an outline, a blip, a backdrop of snow, one space indistinguishable from the next.

Arlo only drives for half a kilometre down the wooded highway before he unexpectedly swerves onto the shoulder and puts the car in park. He grips the steering wheel tight.

Dad? Isaiah asks softly. Is everything okay?

Arlo Bloom breaks into a sob. Whatever these feelings are—pain or guilt or worry—they erupt out of him in bursts, shaking his body like hiccups. It's the only time Isaiah has ever seen his father cry. Father Bloom, who has perfected the art of public composure. Father Bloom, who is always in complete control.

Do you have a bird too? Isaiah wants to ask. Is the flapping too loud?

1964 - 1970

James Lovesee doesn't sleep in his father's lighthouse. The two of them move to Port Peter when James is thirteen, and on the first night, he hears the old building wake from hibernation.

He sits by the lit fireplace in the living room while Alexander Lovesee rewires the beacon atop the lookout, a mile of spiral staircase between them.

And as the damp wood in the fireplace pops and cracks and the northeast wind from Lake Ligeia hisses through the gaps in the aged but sturdy lighthouse stone, James hears another sound. Low and steady. Rhythmic. He feels it through the floor, pounding in the soles of his feet. In the palms of his hands when he touches the walls. In each step of the staircase. In the railing. A beat. A pulse. Alive.

He trips on his way up the stairs, and he is panting by the time he reaches his father at the top. Alexander doesn't acknowledge his young son's presence.

The lighthouse is alive, James whispers, turning to look behind him, as if the building itself might be listening.

Should I kill it for you? Alexander asks.

We can't stay here, James says. Dad—please.

Alexander coughs. He spits out over the lookout's edge. James watches the phlegm fall out of view.

Tell me, Jamie, Alexander says. If I had a lighthouse and a boy, and I could only keep one, which do you think I would choose?

James has long been accustomed to his father's questions. Life with Alexander Lovesee is like a perpetual pop quiz. You know there are going to be questions, but you can never quite prepare.

But this answer doesn't take long. James has always been rather useless. His father tries taking him hunting, but he faints at the smell of blood. He can't lift large fishing nets with his twig arms. He can't hold tools in his shaky fingers. He can't even get his estranged mother in Toronto to answer his calls.

The only thing James Lovesee has that is of use to anyone is his photographic memory. When his father asks him for a paring knife, James knows that it is on the second shelf in the back shed, behind a plastic container of dead daffodil bulbs. When he closes his eyes, he can see his old house in Minden with perfect clarity. Red shingles. Yellow bricks. A lilac tree out front, bent at its centre like a man mid-bow.

James Lovesee is only worth what he can remember, which isn't worth very much at all.

You would choose the lighthouse, James says softly.

Alexander Lovesee tells his son that if he's so *uncomfortable* in the lighthouse, he can sleep outside. He doesn't think that James will sprint back down the stairs and drag his bare twin mattress from his new bedroom out the back door, through the mud, all the way to the tiny tool shed. The shed is dark and damp and smells of rotting wood and rust, but it is most certainly not alive, which is good enough for James. He sleeps in his raincoat and rain boots, tucked beneath a blue tarp. He drifts off to the sound of lake water sloshing against the cliffside, and wind like a flute song through a long crack in the shed's door. And something else in the air. Something—melodic. Singing? No. He must be dreaming that.

Little by little, James makes the tool shed a more habitable bedroom. He nails insulation to the walls in blue tufts, and he buys a quilt from the thrift store in town. He finds an oil lamp to light the space at night. He steals things from inside the lighthouse, his father's things: a yellow pillow off the couch; a woven area rug from the bathroom; a large fishing net, strung from one side of the shed to the other like a canopy, in which to store the blankets and pillows during the day. And books. Encyclopedias. War of 1812 journals. Anatomy textbooks. From the library. From the drugstore. From yard sales. From cardboard boxes on the roadside that read *FREE*.

James Lovesee sleeps in the tool shed until he is nineteen. At dawn he helps his father drag the fishing nets to shore, and during the day he goes to school at Lakeview, and in the evenings he climbs down the cliffs and walks along the shoreline of Lake Ligeia and listens for the Bird songs riding the summer wind, and when the sun sets he joins his father at the lighthouse lookout and helps him man the beacon. But when the moon sits plump and high in the night sky like a peach ripe enough to pick, James retreats to his shed, with his blankets and his books.

One night, the Bird song keeps James awake. The melodies are normally akin to a white noise in the air. A faint chorus of soft voices that could be mistaken for the rustling of tree branches or wind through chimes. James can light a match to soften a beeswax candle and pinch off two pieces of warm wax to plug his ears. And the singing ceases. And the world outside of the tool shed could be the idea of a world. The memory of it.

But James hears the singing through the wax earplugs tonight. It is rustling. Not wind. It isn't a chorus, but a single song with a single singer. And it isn't outside in the memory of the world beyond the tool shed—it is here, right now. Inside James's head.

He follows the song into the trees, down the wooded trail behind his father's live-in lighthouse, over roots and through thickets of dead pine branches, through the darkness of the trees, until he reaches an open clearing atop the cliffside. He can see the lighthouse far off, now, on the other side of the cliffs—a slice of Lake Ligeia between both rock faces. And he can see a woman, sitting on the cliff's edge, her feet dangling over the dark green water below. He hears splashing in the water, and owls in the trees above, but mostly, he hears the woman's voice—sweet like honey to the soul.

He walks closer, and she stops singing midnote. She turns and stares. He breaks the silence first.

Were you the one singing?

SEPTEMBER 2008

Felicity Bloom cannot stop scratching at her skin. The full-body itch has persisted for several weeks. In the crooks of her arms and on the back of her neck and in between her fingers and on the soles of her feet. She scratches so hard that her rounded nails leave little blood spots and long red lines. She soaks in lukewarm baths with baking soda and oatmeal—an old remedy her father taught her—but only finds relief for a few hours at a time.

During choir practice, she scratches herself with her tuning wand, with her crucifix necklace, with one corner of the hard plastic binder she keeps her sheet music in. The choir singers and Devin, the teenaged organ scholar, eye her with suspicion, but Felicity's need for relief outweighs her shame.

At St. Andrew's back in Minden, the servers and sub-deacon would gossip if she accidentally wore white socks with her black shoes during mass. She had a reputation to uphold there: the vicar's wife, the choir director, the cantor. Arlo's standards meant that the St. Andrew's high altar candlesticks were always polished, the lavabo towels and purificators were ironed smooth, and every liturgical object was in its proper position. Felicity and Isaiah were held to the same standard of holiness—not a hair out of place.

But St. Paul's in Port Peter feels different somehow, or perhaps Felicity herself feels different. Maybe in the empty autumn of this tourist town, she cares less about how she is perceived. Maybe she never really cared at all, and all this time, she made herself perfect because she was afraid. Arlo hasn't laid a hand on her in years because she hasn't given him a reason to, but the potential has always existed, like driving past a smoking wreck on the highway and thinking, If I'm not careful, that could easily be me.

The guilt sits on her like the dark wool church skirt that worsens her itch. Because Isaiah is the smoking wreck. Her potential is his reality. Every day.

Part of her is convinced that she is less afraid because there is less of a threat. That Port Peter has calmed her husband somehow. Or maybe aging has given her perspective, and her fear was illogical from the beginning.

Both answers bring her enough momentary peace to protect her from the shameful truth: she feels safer because she is no longer the only woman Arlo wants to control. She doesn't have to be perfect to avoid getting hurt—she just needs to be better than Georgia. That way, when Arlo's pent-up anger can no longer be contained, Georgia will get hurt instead of her.

Felicity is thankful, though, that things have yet to reach that point. Georgia doesn't take the pain meant for Felicity—she takes only the pleasure.

Georgia and Felicity and Arlo continue to meet on Thursday mornings, when Isaiah is at his Bible study and Elsie is working at Buck Deco. They eat breakfast together in the vicarage before they have their fun.

It doesn't take long for the Blooms' facade of perfection to deteriorate in front of Georgia. Felicity and Arlo's marriage is one perpetual argument, each fight picking up where the last one left off. They argue every time Georgia comes over.

They argue about Felicity's sigh that was just a sigh and how quickly or slowly Arlo unbuttoned his shirt, which always turns into an argument about Felicity being intentionally ignorant and Arlo being intentionally provocative.

And yet, each fight ends the same way. Arlo and Georgia on the carpet, fucking with a desperation that Felicity and Arlo never feel together. Felicity splayed out in the queen-sized bed that she normally has to share, Mary Janes kicked off, knee-length dress hiked up, stockings ripped open by her own hand, touching herself in a way that Arlo would never know how to.

It isn't the perfect fantasy. There are pauses, during which Georgia will look to Felicity for affirmation that she is doing what she is supposed to. Georgia has more stamina than Arlo, who sometimes cannot get hard and sometimes finishes in minutes, leaving Georgia flushed but unable to hide her agitation. Georgia gags once after Arlo kisses her. You taste like cigarettes, she says. Felicity covers her mouth with her hand to hide her laughter, and Arlo re-dresses in fuming silence.

One morning, Arlo realizes halfway through that he is late for an appointment with a parishioner for a confession. Felicity expects a glare and a pointed insult, but he blames Georgia instead.

Some of us real fucking adults have commitments to keep, he mutters under his breath, and Georgia grins, under the impression that this is somehow part of the event, an act meant to degrade her a little but leave her craving him.

Maybe you should keep track of your commitments better, she says, smiling, and Felicity stops breathing mid-inhale.

Arlo flexes the fingers in his right hand. He looks at Georgia the way he looks at Isaiah. The look conveys that nothing she says can prevent what happens next.

But just when Felicity expects Arlo to hit her, he walks away. And Felicity exhales. And Georgia chuckles, unaware of the miracle that has just occurred.

Felicity spends September watching Georgia. She is in the vicarage cleaning the kitchen or printing church leaflets in Arlo's study or running a small group on a particular book of the Bible in the living room when Georgia arrives to spend time with Isaiah. It is easy to eavesdrop on their conversations from five feet away. Anyone would do such a thing, especially for the well-being of their son. Felicity isn't confident that Georgia is appropriate company for Isaiah. She tells herself that she is listening so that she can determine if Georgia is a bad influence, filling her son's mind with outlandish ideas.

So far, nothing scandalous has occurred. Georgia and Isaiah mostly talk about mundane things. They ask one another questions as if they were at a job interview. If you could be a colour, which would you be and why? What is your greatest weakness? What time of day were you born? Felicity is positive that Arlo's home-schooling has socially stunted her son.

It makes Felicity nervous when the two of them talk about university. There is a version of Isaiah that would thrive at Trinity—the persona that he puts on around other parishioners. Around his father. Pious and gracious and perfect at all that he does. Then there is the real Isaiah, one that only Felicity sees. The Isaiah who reads Anne Carson in secret and writes his own poetry in the margins of his Bible study workbooks. This Isaiah questions the structures around him. He allows himself to eat too much food and sleep far too late and consider what it is he wants. This Isaiah would be miserable at seminary.

Felicity's interest in Georgia begins as a small thing and grows so gradually that by the time Felicity pays it any mind, it is large enough to cause her discomfort. This girl, the daughter of Arlo's high school best friend, has somehow captivated both Felicity's husband and her son.

Felicity was never quite brave like that at twenty-one. Beautiful. Brazen. Felicity can see it in Georgia's face, but she cannot empathize with it. It isn't something Felicity has ever experienced herself. Is it because of her marriage? Her pregnancy? Her grief after Roselyn's death? It hardly matters now.

Felicity is baking braided rosemary bread one morning when she sees Georgia coming in through the back door. She expects Isaiah to shuffle in behind her, but it is just Georgia, in her bare feet and a purple paisley suit jacket with shoulder pads, her honey hair braided and pinned up like a bride.

Whatever it is you're making smells divine, Georgia says. So good it should be illegal. Call the pigs! Alert the FBI! Start up the electric chair!

It's bread, Felicity says. Where is Isaiah?

Church. We had breakfast at Crime Brûlée and then he had to serve with Arlo. He said I could wait here so that we can go out after they're done.

You're always welcome here, Felicity says. I'll be in the kitchen finishing the loaves if you need—

Could I watch you?

Felicity frowns.

Watch me?

Make bread, I mean. I don't need to know how to make it myself. You can buy bread at the store that's like, the same.

I don't ever have to *make* bread. I just want to watch you. Like watching a cooking show.

A pause.

Alright, Felicity says. But it won't be very exciting.

Georgia sits cross-legged on the kitchen counter while Felicity takes the first loaf out of the oven to cool. She removes the cloth covering the bowl of dough for the second loaf. She takes off her wedding band and engagement ring, placing them on top of the microwave. She dusts her hands with flour and begins to knead air bubbles out of the dough. Fold after fold. It deflates and inflates again and again.

Felicity?

Yes?

Am I the first woman you and Arlo have—had breakfast with? Together?

Felicity tries to act as if the question doesn't faze her, even though she feels silly, now, like some facade of maturity and seasoned sexuality has disappeared.

Yes, she admits.

She punches the air out of the dough with more force. Georgia is quiet, considering this.

And Arlo hasn't ever had breakfast with anyone other than you, she says finally.

It is more of a statement than a question.

What makes you think that? Felicity asks.

It just seems like—like you tell him what to do with me because otherwise, he wouldn't know what to do.

Do I seem like I would know what to do?

You do, Georgia says. With another woman, I mean.

Felicity is over-kneading the dough. The bread is already ruined. Oh well.

I didn't mean to assume, Georgia adds.

Would you know what to do with another woman, Georgia? Felicity asks.

Georgia nods.

Men are like soft serve ice cream, she says. Soft serve is good, obviously. It doesn't cost much either. But you have to eat it really fast because if you don't it melts and gets all over you. Women are like—artisan gelato. You can eat gelato with that little spoon and savour the taste, and each bite is the best bite you've ever had.

Then why would you ever choose soft serve over gelato? Felicity asks.

I get cravings for soft serve sometimes, Georgia says.

I had a girlfriend before I was married, Felicity says. Roselyn.

Were you in love?

Very much so, yes.

Did she break your heart?

She shot herself.

Silence. Felicity sighs.

She was Arlo's sister, she continues. Someone in the congregation walked in on us and told everyone else. Our Vicar found out. Asked to meet with me one-on-one, without Rose. I thought he'd make me recite Romans 1:26-28 or something, or kick my father and I out of the church. But he made me coffee, and we talked about music: mass settings and Medieval polyphony and arrangement ideas I had for the O Antiphons the following Advent. Near the end of our chat, he asked me if I looked up to Roselyn. He talked about power. He brought up our age difference. What if I had been caught with her brother? I asked. They're the same age. Would we still be talking about power? No, he said. I doubt it. I saw Roselyn once, after that. Just one time.

And her hand is at Roselyn's locket. She runs her thumb over the blue bird.

I'm sorry, Georgia says softly.

Felicity waves her off. Clears her throat.

Do you want to see the bread before I brush it?

Georgia slides herself off the counter and peers over Felicity's shoulder. The rosemary loaf is fully braided, and now it must be brushed with egg yolk before going into the oven.

Very fucking artisanal, Georgia says.

Felicity snickers.

Like your hair, she said, pointing to Georgia's pinned braids.

I've been told my hair is delicious, Georgia says.

When Felicity runs a hand across the back of her neck to scratch the itch below her own hair, wound in a tight bun, she feels something tiny sticking out of her skin. Firm in the middle, like a twig, but light and soft on the edges. A feather.

When she brings her hand back, the tips of her fingers are red with blood.

Shit, Georgia says. Did you cut yourself separating the dough?

I must've, the bird in Felicity's skull whispers.

I must've, Felicity mutters.

After Georgia has gone out with Isaiah, and Isaiah has returned home, and the Blooms have done their evening prayer and eaten dinner, Felicity walks back down to the beach behind the vicarage. The tide is high, and there isn't much room to stand in the sand without getting wet. The August wind sends small waves towards shore. A full moon illuminates the green-brown water of Lake Ligeia, making it look almost emerald. Crickets chirp from dead foliage.

Despite the wind, the air is humid. Felicity sweats in her black long-sleeved dress and black stockings and dress shoes. Her dark hair sticks to the back of her neck. When she is positive that she is alone, she strips off her clothes and folds them in a neat little pile near the wooden steps on the hill. She keeps Roselyn's bird locket on. She has not taken it off since it was given to her. Not for her wedding. Not for Isaiah's birth. Not now.

The water is warm, yet refreshing on her skin. Felicity feels algae squish between her toes. As soon as she is far enough, she dunks below the surface, and her hair floats above her as if she is hanging upside down. She feels guilty, in a way, that she is enjoying herself this much.

Submerged, Felicity tries to see how long she can hold her breath. When she was six, she could hold it for a full minute. At what age do one's lungs begin to die, slowly? Is she old enough to already be dying? Thirty-seven is young to some, but old to others. How long does it take a body to die? How long does it take a body to drown? Three minutes? Two? She read it somewhere once, but she doesn't remember.

Thirty seconds in, the singing starts.

It is warped. Like when Felicity used to sing into the electric fan to change her voice. Still, Felicity can tell that it is indeed singing. A chorus of voices, performing a melody without words.

Her head breaks the surface of the water. A deep inhale.

The singing has stopped. But she just heard it a moment ago—why would the voices halt so suddenly? It was such a beautiful song, she thinks. She must hear more.

She dives beneath the water again and, sure enough, the singing returns. Still muffled. Still far off. But it is real.

Felicity repeats this process over and over. Diving down to hear the song. Coming up for air, wondering where it has gone. It would not make sense if—no. That isn't possible. The singing cannot be coming from the bottom of the lake.

She wants to hear it clearer. Closer. She wants to see who could be singing such a comforting, soothing tune. How long might it take to swim to the bottom if she kicked as hard as she could? How deep is Lake Ligeia? Is it worth finding out? Is it not? She is convinced that it is. She is more convinced of this than she has been of anything else in her entire life.

And she is almost six feet down, swimming, swimming, the singing, the singing, louder, louder, clearer, when she remembers Isaiah. If Felicity left, her son would be motherless. Alone with his father. The image of him is so clear in her mind. His dark curls. Deep brown eyes. The kindness with which he treats everyone he meets, no matter how much unrest he experiences at home. She cannot leave him. She will not.

She swims back to the surface, gasping for air when she breaks through the water. She listens. Crickets. Waves. Her breathing, heavy and laboured. No singing.

Back on shore, she puts her clothes on before she is dry, and they stick to her uncomfortably. She stays on the beach a while longer, cross-legged in the sand and rocks, watching the small waves curl up and drop down.

She stops. The singing is back, but not as it was before. It is audibly louder. Brighter. Somewhere out on the lake rather than beneath it. It is gorgeous. Serene. Everything Felicity wants. Everything she needs.

And then, it isn't singing, but speaking.

Come back.

A woman's voice. Desperate and cracked, as if spoken through tears.

Come back.

It sounds like—no. Impossible. Georgia is home in bed.

Come back, Felicity.

But—it *is* Georgia Jackson's voice. Felicity was just with her. She is so certain. She looks around her on the beach. Did Georgia follow her? Here? At this time of night?

Come back. Please, Felicity. Come back.

Georgia? Felicity calls out. Georgia?

The voice doesn't answer. The night air doesn't answer. Lake Ligeia doesn't answer.

Suddenly, Felicity is crying. Georgia's voice is so loud—so real. It can't be real. It is. It can't be. Felicity is home, isn't she? She was born in Port Peter. She lives in Port Peter. She is steps away from the vicarage. From her family.

Where is Georgia?

Where is home?

It stops. Without warning.

And then there is a tickle in Felicity's throat. She tries to clear it. Ahem. Ahem. She coughs, and she cannot stop coughing, cannot catch her breath, and the coughing turns to choking, it isn't just an itch, not just a tickle, but something scratching the inside of her throat, and she gags, out, out, and she is so desperate to stop the sensation that she reaches a hand inside her mouth, her fingers feeling around for whatever is there, another gag, and she feels something wet and soft and she yanks it out, and she isn't positive what she is choking on until she pulls a long white feather from her throat, wet with blood.

SEPTEMBER 1970

In the days and weeks after James's night with Kind in the lighthouse, he skips helping his father with the beacon to watch the Birds on their nightly swim at the base of the cliff. He listens to them sing and laugh and debate about poetry and philosophy and morality. He never interrupts them—never makes his presence known. He knows that it isn't his place. Still, he watches Kind the closest. He watches her sickness start, and her belly swell, and he knows that he is to blame.

He eventually refuses to help his father with the Bird traps. They're like us, he argues. They're people. It's unjust.

Alexander Lovesee regards his son closely. He seems to chew on his words before he spits them out.

You knocked one up? he asks.

James says nothing. He looks out to the water as if it might answer for him. Then, he nods.

Alexander laughs.

You know what they'll do to the baby, right?

Silence. Alexander rolls his eyes.

Your kid won't be one of them, he says. It'll be like you. Like a man. And they'll do what they do to all men.

She won't.

She's death incarnate, Alexander says. That's her purpose on earth: to fuck. And to kill. And to feed. And you gave her exactly what she wanted.

A pause.

I hope you get to see her do it, he adds. I hope you never forget.

JUNE 1971

Kind skips the group swim. She climbs up to the cliffside and tries to find the trail back to the lighthouse, but she gets lost in the woods. It is dark, even in the middle of the day, darker than she remembers. No sunlight—just treetops. She wanders around for hours until singing in her head pulls her back home.

The next day, Kind tries again. She does this for months, as her belly swells and her hips widen, and her ankles become plump. Her hair grows thicker. Her pace is slower, more laboured. Her searches become shorter and shorter. She cannot find the lighthouse.

She gives birth to a girl in Lake Ligeia, surrounded by a circle of Birds. Lila grips Kind's shoulders from behind. Two other Birds hold Kind steady, and another brings the baby up to breathe. It hurts. The adrenalin does not make it painless. It is just Kind, with all her shortcomings, bleeding on the rocks beneath her God's star-filled sky, doing what needs to be done.

Shrieking. The baby is covered in blood and mucus. She is still attached to her mother by the thick yellow umbilical cord, and she has a head full of hair. She wails and wails as if she is belting a hymn—something sacred and splendid for all the world to hear.

Lila takes the baby—holds her out for Kind to see. Kind looks back at Lila, full of fear.

Lila cuts the umbilical cord with the ridges of a sharp rock—Birds are very resourceful creatures. She swaddles the girl in an old dress. The girl's skin is bright red.

Kind gives birth to the placenta next, red and purple and shaped like a jellyfish.

Kind is crying. She is shivering. She is smiling. Lila hands the baby to Kind, and Kind looks at her with an expression of shock, the death of her old life fresh in her mind. She cradles her loosely, as if she is holding something that could hurt her. The baby stops crying—looks up at Kind with curiosity.

Kind spends weeks after the birth inspecting her daughter, trying to see herself in her daughter's eyes and facial features. The baby has dark hair and dark eyes. Dark like the very bottom of the lake. Kind thinks about the way Lila looked at her own baby, about the odd, inseparable, instantaneous love that mothers are supposed to have for their children, but Kind does not feel such love. When she looks at her daughter, she does not feel anything at all.

SEPTEMBER 2008

Georgia is on her fourth cigarette, watching bats zip above the maple tree in her front yard, when she sees Isaiah walking up her street. It is that hard-to-see-anything time between dusk and night, but Georgia can spot his head of brown curls and nervous gait—like he's trying not to wake a guard dog that doesn't exist. He has a reusable green IGA grocery bag hanging off one shoulder.

Isaiah waves, but when he raises his hand, the bag falls off his shoulder and into the dusty driveway gravel.

Georgia has spent the last two months getting to know Isaiah. When she isn't working with her mom at Buck Deco or sleeping with Felicity and Arlo, she is with him, walking the boardwalk or walking through the trails off County Road Five or walking to M&M Meat Shops to eat free samples of meatballs in sweet sauce or walking to the Tim Hortons on the strip so that they have Timbits to eat while they walk somewhere else. It is both refreshing and strange to spend time with a man who hasn't called her a bitch or tried to sleep with her. She can't quite wrap her head around it, and spends a lot of time trying to figure out what his ulterior motive might be.

Isaiah Bloom thanks every cashier he meets and prays the angelus every time an ambulance passes by and tips too much for lunch at Crime Brûlée and picks up trash everywhere he goes to leave it cleaner than when he arrived. Georgia has never heard him swear or talk back to either of his parents, and his clothes are beautiful and boring, and he cares too much about how clean they are. No one is just *that* nice. Not for no reason.

He's also so clumsy that he's got a new bruise every time she sees him, and he can't tell a story in a straight line, and he has seen so little TV throughout his life that he doesn't even know what a house hippo is or that Good Things Grow in Ontario, and he lost his virginity at Bible camp when he was sixteen to a girl named Gabriella and got banned from ever going back, and he reads Carson and Sexton and Plath but pretends to his parents that he doesn't.

Isaiah has given Georgia the kind of friendship that she doesn't realize she needs until she has it, and now it is an integral part of her life.

And as she comes to care for Isaiah more and more, the guilt of keeping her arrangement with his parents from him increases. It reminds her that no matter how much love is shown to her, she doesn't deserve it. She chooses herself, over and over, every Thursday morning.

Isaiah is out of breath by the time he reaches Georgia's porch.

I brought you plays, he says. I got them when my father and I were in the city buying new beeswax candles and looking at vestments. I'm going to do a little show and tell for you.

Please do.

Isaiah's Play Selections

• *Perfect Pie* by Judith Thompson

• *Aphra* by Rose Scollard, Nancy Jo Cullen, and
  Alexandria Patience

• *Dried Flowers* by Maryjane Cruise

• *Willful Acts* by Margaret Hollingsworth

They're all written by women—Canadian women, Isaiah
continues. The bookstore clerk recommended them to me.
Maybe you'll be friends with all these people one day.

Georgia makes two mugs of instant coffee and pops a
bag of popcorn. The two of them eat burnt popcorn and lie
on their stomachs on the front porch while attempting to
write their own play. Georgia scribbles their ideas on printer
paper in silver Sharpie.

And the siren orgy has to be called *The Bodyssey*, Georgia
says.

And the men can be tied to a maypole with ribbons, instead of tied to a mast, Isaiah says.

And when we're under water, we should flood the stage
in dark green light.

Or the whole theatre.

Brilliant.

We should think about the Bird costumes.

The Bird costumes are the most important part.

What if they aren't even actors? What if we made incred-
ibly elaborate shadow puppets?

Do you know how to make shadow puppets?

No. Do you?

Not even a little bit. We'll find the best shadow puppe-teers on earth.

How would we afford them?

We don't hire them—we hire their children, who have learned the craft through osmosis. Their playful energy will make the shadows more alive.

Absolutely.

And you'll write a book of poetry that's basically a con-cept album from the perspective of the sirens, and in the six months before we open the show the first poems from the book will get published in magazines and journals and even printed out and taped onto walls at street corners in the city, and then a month before the show the whole book will come out with some avant-garde indie press and we'll hide copies everywhere, like sticking out of storm drains in the suburbs and behind boxes of Raisin Bran at the grocery store and in the pews at St. Paul's behind *Common Praise*, and on opening night you and I will wear suits with feather embroidery all down the sleeves and people will be like, Are those angels?

And there should also be a kindergarten choir singing sea shanties and doing Gregorian chants. In a minor chord. So it's spooky.

We might have to work together for the rest of our lives after that, Isaiah. People will expect us to. We'll be bound to one another stronger than siblings or lovers and then our wives will grow resentful of how much time we spend together.

We could use it to everyone's advantage, Isaiah says. We could babysit each other's kids.

Georgia begins to laugh. It's contagious, and Isaiah can't help but laugh with her. They laugh until their stomachs hurt, like they've just done hundreds of sit-ups.

I don't want kids, Georgia says.

Me neither, Isaiah says.

Inside, mounted buck heads line the walls. Their antlers are full of objects. Hung coats and hunting hats and a big blue-and-white cooler with three cracked wheels. A massive bearskin rug covers the living room. A green-and-red plaid couch and a big TV that Georgia has never been able to lift by herself.

Georgia takes Isaiah to her bedroom, where the walls are covered in torn-out book pages. A few movie posters are tacked over top: *Pretty Woman*, *Dancer in the Dark*, the 1996 *Romeo + Juliet*. Isaiah points to the *Matilda* poster above Georgia's bed.

This is the one with the witch girl, right? he asks.

Bullshit. There's no way you haven't seen *Matilda*.

Never.

They sit cross-legged on Georgia's bedroom carpet and start to watch *Matilda* on her little pink TV. Georgia is silent until halfway through the previews.

Matilda is maybe probably my favourite movie, she says quietly.

Really?

I guess so.

I feel honoured that you're sharing it with me then, Isaiah says. Why is it your favourite?

I think it's because Matilda, like, learns to read when she's really young. And she doesn't just love reading. She needs it. She uses to it to survive, you know? And no matter what is happening at home, how alone she feels, she always has those stories, those other worlds that she can escape to, where she can do and be anything that she wants. There's this scene where the child actress playing Matilda changes because Matilda gets older, and they show her aging while hauling a wagonful of books around, like books kept being her safe place all those years, like the stories raised her. And that feels like what stories are supposed to do. Maybe you write them for people who are like you—you write the kind of book or play or poem you needed when you were that age or in that situation. Or maybe you write to show people that there's hope despite all the bad shit in the world that you see every day. And what happens is that people who you wouldn't even expect to find your story find it, and it helps them in ways you never imagined, with hardships you've never even gone through yourself. The best stories are like that: personal and universal at the same time. They find the people like you and they connect you with the people who aren't like you. Herman Melville didn't write *Moby-Dick* for Matilda, but it helped her anyway, and now they're sharing that story across time, in this weird way. In this divine way. And now I'm sharing in the story too. And you're sharing it with me. Stories like that make me believe in God.

Georgia turns her head and sees that Isaiah's eyes are red and watering. He looks back at her, and he smiles, and he nods.

Yes, he says finally. I feel that way, too.

They stay on the bedroom carpet long after the movie is over, and as the two of them talk and read, Georgia feels like they are knit together by a thousand tiny threads, stitched slowly and carefully over the last few months. And Georgia has not noticed until now—until the stiches have combined the two of them completely.

I pretend a lot, Isaiah says.

Yeah, Georgia says. I pretend a lot too.

And I'm really tired.

Yeah.

They should convert every pay phone booth on every street corner into a place where you can go to say things out loud that you can't say anywhere else, Georgia says. Like a panic room, but for the truth. So people can get it out somewhere.

Who's they?

The Green Party. It would be a good campaign point.

What would you say, Isaiah asks, if you had somewhere to say it?

I would say that I'm pretty sure my mom's old boyfriend Mark is my dad, Georgia says.

Oh.

He used to jerk off in front of me. When we were alone watching movies. He did other stuff too. I don't remember really. It's sort of like trying to remember a dream.

Isaiah doesn't say anything. He nods.

Is destiny a thing in the Bible? Georgia asks. Like, when something happens to you that's your fault, and you're different after, bad different, and your life is destined to be the aftermath of that, no matter what you do?

Not really, Isaiah says.

A pause.

And it wasn't your fault, Georgia, he adds.

Thanks, Isaiah.

After a long pause, Isaiah speaks again.

I would say that I'm nineteen years old and I'm afraid of my father, Isaiah says. Afraid enough that I dream about him and wake up screaming. And when I'm out by myself somewhere, like walking down a street, I think that every man who passes me on a bike or glances at me through the window of a car or jogs near me on the sidewalk is him, just for a split second, like I'm hallucinating or something, and then I forget how to breathe.

Georgia doesn't know what to say. Isaiah continues.

I'd tell the truth booth that for most of my life, I thought everyone else's fathers ripped all the covers off their books when they accidentally spilled a cup of apple juice and gave them concussions breaking down the doors to their bedrooms and called them worthless pieces of shit for not taking holiday traditions seriously enough and spat in their faces like they were less than nothing. And that even though I wake up every day afraid that he's going to kill me, I love him. And I would let him do anything to me if he needed to.

It doesn't take long for shame to fill Georgia. Like lake water bloating her stomach. Making her ribs ache. Rising, rising, filling her lungs, her throat, she can taste it now, the algae, and the mud, and the grit of the sand in her teeth, and she tries to inhale but she can't. She is sleeping with a man who hurts his son. Isaiah has cut himself open for Georgia, baring his most terrifying secret, and Georgia is in an intimate relationship with the person who causes him the most harm.

I'm sorry, Georgia whispers.

And she is.

I think I have to leave, Isaiah continues. And I think I should go to school for something I actually want.

His eyes are shut as he speaks.

What I mean is—I don't know if I'm going to get in. Probably not. But I—I'm moving. I need to move away. I'm going to go to the city either way. And you should come with me.

You want me to live with you? Georgia asks. In the city?

We could be roommates, he says. If you want. And you could write more monologues. Whole plays. Or whatever else you wanted to write like anything and everything like obituaries and movie scripts and a trilogy. And I could write my poetry and we could have our own books. In a bookcase. Or two bookcases, one for each of us. And a pet bird if you wanted. Or no pets. And you would never have to wear shoes inside the apartment. You hate shoes—it would be perfect.

It would be perfect, Georgia thinks. The arrangement with Arlo and Felicity won't last forever anyway. They'll be bored of her soon enough. It felt really good being desired, or wanted, or used, but she thought it might become something else—something that wasn't just about the sex. Something about who she is and her brain and what a life with her might look like if you looked at her and really fucking tried to imagine it like wow I could grocery shop with her I could do my taxes with her I could sit on a porch in rocking chairs with her and she would be okay with that life. But it has never been that, has it? She feels stupid for thinking that it ever could be. Or maybe she has known the whole time and was just lying to herself, like how she is lying to Isaiah and her mom like the fucking liar she is, and maybe she can't even help it maybe she doesn't even have a truth anymore because her personality is entirely made of lies.

But being with Isaiah feels like the truth. It is real. It is enough.

I think I would like that a lot, she says.

APRIL 1972

When the girl is old enough to crawl, Kind takes her to the cliffside. She lets the baby squirm and writhe in the grass like she's trying to get out of a cocoon, growing wings for the first time.

Lila joins Kind on the cliffside. The baby picks at dandelions and drools and shakes her tiny fists. Kind tries to get her to say real words by repeating a choice few repeatedly: *Mom. Milk. Lake.* The baby cannot speak, though Kind often wonders if she can, just chooses not to.

Lila and Kind watch the other Birds moving freely in the water below. Kind's body was for housing and now it is for feeding. She is a commodity. She tries to remember when her body was her own: her hips aligned the way they were created, her breasts small enough to cup in her palms. Suddenly, she finds herself becoming angry. She wants to be her own again. She wants to be her own.

Did you regret it? At first? Kind asks.

Lila keeps her eyes on the lake. She squints in the sun.

Regret what?

This, Kind clarifies. When you first had your baby. Did you wish you could take it back somehow?

A pause.

No, Lila says.

She runs her hand along the grass.

I loved it, she continues. I couldn't imagine being anyone else.

Lila finally turns to face Kind.

You understand, right?

No, Kind says. Not really.

Lila stops. It is quiet. No cooing, no shuffling. She glances at the space on the grass behind them. She does a double take.

Kind, she says quietly.

Kind turns. The grass behind Lila and Kind is empty. The baby is gone.

Both Birds stand, and Kind opens her mouth to call out, but then she realizes—her baby does not have a name. How do you find a baby who does not have a name?

Kind looks to Lila in desperation.

Lila's eyes scan the cliffside, the water below, the sky above. Nothing. She begins to sing, shriek, scream, all three sounds at once. The noise is deafening.

Kind's mind cannot comprehend this moment. She cannot be here. In this place. In this body. Her body that used to be home to her baby. Her baby that was here. Right here. And now? Somewhere else. Nowhere. All of it is too much to bear.

And suddenly, a flapping starts behind her eyes, tickling her eardrums. The sound of chirping coming from—inside her? That can't be right.

It isn't real singing. Not one of the other Birds that Kind lives with below the lake. It is birdsong. A goldfinch, perhaps. No, a kinglet. A ruby-crowned kinglet. At this time of year?

The kinglet in Kind's head flaps and flaps. It absorbs this moment in time while Kind cannot. It remembers.

1972 - 1978

James Lovesee finds his infant daughter by accident. He walks to the cliffside clearing to watch the solar eclipse, and as he emerges from the wooded trail, he sees a girl barely big enough to crawl. All folds—tiny arms and legs. A head of dark chestnut hair and big brown eyes. His eyes.

And farther out, he can see Kind, and another woman—another Bird—lounging beside her.

James watches his daughter in the grass, babbling to no one in particular, and he thinks about his mother in Toronto who doesn't return his calls, and he thinks about the physical sensation that he gets each time he presses his ear up to the receiver and waits—nerves like moths but with sound instead of light, each ring more delicious than the last—optimistic that perhaps, this time, something will come over his mother, a parental instinct, a blood-linked love, a yearning for connection, and she will finally answer—and then that fifth and final ring, the one before her answering machine message begins, and the moths in his stomach retreat and resign themselves to the fact that they will never fly again.

And he can't be the one to inflict that kind of pain on his daughter. He knows it is selfish, but if he had to choose one parent to do the inflicting, he would choose Kind.

The choice no longer feels hypothetical. It is real. It is now.

He does not remember lifting his daughter up out of the grass. He does not remember the running, thin birch branches whipping his face, down the wooded trail. He only remembers his lungs, empty. His legs, cramped. His hand, clamped over the baby's little mouth to keep her from crying out. Stopping under the shadow of an old dead pine because his body could go no farther. And Kind's screaming—ear-splitting, even from a mile away.

James sleeps in his father's lighthouse that night. He does not think that a tool shed is an appropriate place for a baby. His father shows James how to hold her, swaying ever so slightly. He bathes her in the kitchen sink while James watches and takes note of how to lift her head and how warm the water should be. He dresses her in James's baby clothes. He feeds her red grapes and slices of banana and small bites of cooked muskie fish. James eyes the baby nervously, as if she might sprout wings and fly away.

Shouldn't she be crying for her mother? James asks.

It seems you got lucky, Alexander says. She carries herself with a certain felicity.

James fits the living room couch with thick quilts, and when night falls, his daughter falls asleep on his chest, mouth open, tiny breaths like hiccups, and James watches her breathe. He worries that if he doesn't watch, the breathing might stop. He can hear the lighthouse breathing, too. Creaks in the walls and the ceiling. That same heartbeat he heard at thirteen years old—weaker now, but still there.

The baby smiles. Even in sleep, she cannot contain her felicity.

It makes sense at first for James and his daughter to stay living in the Port Peter lighthouse, where they have food and advice from Alexander, who always seems to know things about parenting that James doesn't, like to bathe Felicity in oatmeal when she gets chicken pox and to give her a rubber spatula end to chew on while her teeth grow in and what she means to say when she seems to babble incoherently.

But what James gains in knowledge, he loses through the near-constant anxiety of wondering where his father's patience with Felicity will end. Each time Alexander Lovesee makes her scrambled eggs for breakfast, or braids her hair, or takes her out by the lake to check his hunting traps, James feels an overwhelming vigilance. A full-body muscle flex in anticipation of imminent cruelty. When will these things, these gestures of love, be used against her?

Everything Alexander Lovesee has ever done for James is on a perpetual list of debts to be paid, incurring interest by the second. Look, his father would say. Look at the groceries I buy you. The hot water in your bath. The clothes on your back. Your reading glasses. Your hiking boots. Your silver filling. Your bed and your sheets and your books and your coffee and the mugs and the records and the school supplies. You're ungrateful. You wouldn't survive a minute without me.

Any moment, Felicity's scrambled eggs and her braids and her rubber boots are bound to be worthy cause to belittle her. To make her feel as though nothing in her life really belongs to her.

When James tells his father that he and Felicity are moving out of the lighthouse, Alexander laughs in his face.

I think I was wrong, he says finally.

About what? James asks.

You should've left the girl with the Birds, he says. She would've been better off.

James says nothing, but deep in his heart, he agrees.

He finds a duplex rental ad in the *Port Peter Review*—the attic of an early-nineteenth-century house up north in Minden, owned by St. Andrew's Anglican Church. St. Andrew's uses the main floor of the house as a parish hall, but they can no longer afford the electricity and water bills for the entire structure. They want tenants who will double as parishioners: quiet, eager, and, of course, Anglican.

James has read a pocket-sized ESV Old and New Testament a few times through over the course of his years in the tool shed. It was one of the books he had bought from the thrift store, and in his mind, it operated not unlike any other fantastical narrative. It had men in whale bellies and women turned to pillars of salt and fingers stuck in open wounds without a twinge of pain. A God who was Father, Son, man, not man, ghost, wind, creation, time, beginning, end. Stories have beginnings and ends too, James thinks. It doesn't make them any more real.

But he needs to get out. He needs a place to sleep that isn't alive or a tool shed. His daughter needs to grow up surrounded by good people—the kind of people who give to the poor and eat Sunday dinner at the dining room table and believe in something. Believing in something larger than yourself made you, at the very least, pretend to be good. James can put up with pretending. He can pretend.

The attic apartment in Minden is not alive. It is a tomb of dead things: daddy-long-legs, baby mice, earwigs, dreams of a life somewhere else. The walls of that attic apartment have seen lovers fight and lovers fuck and lovers leave without taking their love with them. They have seen babies born blue and wrapped in white sheets. They have seen unanswered prayers and the prospect of maybe-miracles. They have seen the dead remain dead—without resurrection.

James and Felicity like it that way. It is comforting, some-how, to be in a house without a heartbeat. To hear silence for the very first time.

They are at St. Andrew's almost every single day: for mass and morning prayer and evening prayer and compline and Gregorian evensong and choir practice and serving practice and volunteer bake sales. James wants to keep Felicity busy. He wants to be the best non-believing Anglo-Catholic there ever was so that, no matter what, he and his daughter have a place to live.

They pray to the saints by day and read tarot cards by night. That second life is important to James. Not as im-portant as having a place to live, but important enough to share with his daughter as she grows. The two of them fall into a natural rhythm of sanctity and secrecy, balancing both aspects of themselves like sides of a scale, never adding enough weight to cause abrupt shifts into one lifestyle or the other. Both father and daughter find it difficult to pray, and both find it difficult to fully trust the cards.

And thus they exist in a spiritual purgatory.

OCTOBER 2008

The Jacksons drive through fog and dark down the Highway 85 service road on their way home from Buck Deco. There is no traffic—no tourists. Elsie drives with one hand and searches radio channels with the other.

Georgia has become accustomed to her mother switching between news stations until one of them starts to talk about something unimaginably terrible. A Walmart bomb scare or robbery shootout. A family gone on a boat trip who never returned, lost at sea. Her mother finds calm in sad news. She reads the *Niagara Weekly* obituaries every morning with her coffee. She works in her taxidermy shop on the strip, cleaning dead animals and emptying them and sewing them back up and painting them until they are practically alive again. When she has time to relax, she watches true crime documentaries. Death scares most people, but it does not scare Elsie Jackson.

Mom? Georgia says.

Yeah?

Are you afraid of your dad?

Elsie lowers the radio volume.

Not anymore, she says finally. When he was alive, maybe.

Did you love him?

I did.

But how can you love someone that you're afraid of?

He was nice sometimes. And when he was nice, I kind of forgot that I was afraid… Is this about someone you know?

No, Georgia lies. I was just curious.

I think my mother felt guilty for staying with him, Elsie says. Because of how he treated us. I think she thought that loving someone who hurt other people made her a person who hurt other people by association, or by direct support. But getting into the same bed with someone who hurts your kid is like giving them absolution, again and again, wiping them clean at the end of each day, I forgive you, I forgive you. Then I got pregnant, and my dad told me I had to leave.

Your mom didn't try to convince him to let you stay?

She didn't, no. I'm really grateful that she didn't.

I don't understand.

I couldn't have raised you in that house, Elsie says. You wouldn't have been safe with my dad there. She protected me, and you, by letting us leave.

Georgia wonders if this is the same kind of protecting that Elsie was trying to do when she left Georgia in the laundry basket on the cliffside. The selfish kind.

Do you think she died feeling guilty? Georgia asks.

Probably.

Do you think she feels guilty right now? Like, eternally?

I don't think she feels anything now.

Back home, Elsie and Georgia cover their worn leather couch in pillows and comforters and Elsie puts on a pirated copy of *The Dark Knight*. It's a cam version—filmed in the theatre—so the sound is out of sync, and the screen is sometimes blurry, and Georgia can see the shadows of moviegoers as they find their seats. *The Dark Knight* is so dark that Batman blends into his surroundings in every scene. Georgia and Elsie share a roll of raw cookie dough.

The cam copy is split into two parts. Disk one ends midway through the interrogation scene at GCPD headquarters. It's too dark for Georgia to see Heath Ledger's face while he speaks. How can you miss somebody if you can't even remember what they look like? Georgia can't tell if Heath's Joker is warning Christian Bale or teasing him. These civilized people...they'll eat each other.

But the Jacksons' DVD player doesn't read disk two properly, and while Elsie tries everything in her power to make the disk readable—wiping it down with paper towel and blowing on it like it is hot soup—Georgia is still thinking about absolution by association, how that would mean that she is complicit when Arlo harms Isaiah, and that Felicity is complicit when Arlo harms Isaiah, and that Elsie was complicit when Mark II harmed Georgia, and how complicated it all is, because Georgia knows that her mother loves her, that her mother would never want to hurt her, and Georgia loves Isaiah, in a way, and would never want to hurt him, but Georgia has been hurt, and Isaiah has been hurt, and whatever anyone originally intended or didn't intend doesn't matter anymore. Would the situation be easier to stomach if she had afflicted Isaiah on purpose? If her siren song was meant to draw him to his death? Unintentional harm feels worse, somehow, especially when the only person you want to hurt is yourself, singing a song that only you can hear.

OCTOBER 2008

It is odd to Isaiah how much Port Peter transforms in mid-autumn.

The full St. Paul's congregation that welcomed the Blooms a few months ago has now dwindled to fewer than thirty people, spread out among the various services. Isaiah can infer from his father's mood that the swaths of generous donations have stopped. There are simply fewer parishioners, and those left over are mostly out of work, hoarding what money they have until next summer, when Port Peter will come back to life. Fewer parishioners giving means less spending on things the church needs. A smaller number of parishioners equates to a smaller budget from the diocese—a smaller salary for Arlo. The Blooms start walking everywhere in town to save on gas. They take cans of non-perishables from the church food bank and bring them home when money is too tight for groceries.

Arlo has become a land mine, sensitive to the slightest provocation, and Isaiah walks the field as best he can. He eats boxed stuffing and instant noodles and powdered mashed potatoes without complaint. He apologizes in conversation, even when he has done nothing wrong. He cleans the kitchen before anyone even notices that it is dirty, anticipating things that his father might find irritating. So far, he has been successful in keeping himself from physical harm for the past month—the longest stretch in his life. He's not positive why this is, why his father is more hesitant to lay a hand on him, but he's certain that it won't last long.

Port Peter seems to have a strange effect on all three of the Blooms. When Felicity is supposed to be at church leading a Bible study or supporting Arlo from the pews, she is outside, on her own. She takes the sloped wooden steps down to the beach.

One day, Isaiah follows her. He stays at the top of the hill and watches her sit in the sand below. She stares out at Lake Ligeia's brilliant green water for almost three hours. It is almost as if she is watching over it, like a mother standing over a sleeping baby, waiting for its chest to rise and fall.

Isaiah cannot seem to stop writing. Poems pours out of him—usually about his days spent with Georgia. They see each other so often that there are almost as many poems as days he has lived in Port Peter. It's difficult to find places to write them, at first. His father checks his phone. A notebook would easily be found. He could use scraps—napkins and receipts and the backs of church service leaflets—but eventually, he would run out of places to hide them.

He begins to write his poems in the margins of his books, where Arlo cannot find them. A poem about having lunch at Crime Brûlée. A poem about walking on the shoulder of the service road in the middle of the night, he and Georgia passing a blue raspberry slushie between them. About the boardwalk. About the cave.

It is late in October when Isaiah helps Georgia and her mother set up the taxidermy petting zoo for Port Peter's only cold-weather public event: the Happening in the Park.

A Brief History of the Happening in the Park

*Told second-hand by Isaiah Abel Bloom, who was only half
paying attention when it was explained to him.*

- It's a secular fun fair that's harvest themed, but also summer themed, and it started as a way to raise money to get through the rest of the winter until the tourists come back.

- People dress as giant peaches, even though peaches aren't in season right now. There's a Peach King and a Peach Queen, and they're the mascots, but they bump into things because the eyeholes in the costumes aren't big enough, and sometimes the Peach King passes out from lack of oxygen. Georgia asks to be the Peach Queen every year, but she's always turned down.

- Elsie hosts a taxidermy petting zoo. All the animals are stuffed. Some are even posable. Elsie says it's better than a real petting zoo because the animals don't bite you back, and have you ever gotten to pet a crow or a two-headed snake at a real petting zoo?

- There's popcorn and cotton candy and hot cider. You can also bob for peaches, though Georgia strongly recommends not engaging in that activity unless you really want to get hand, foot, and mouth disease.

The taxidermy animals are stacked in the back of Elsie's Toyota Corolla in a large, frightening pile. Elsie puts the smaller creatures like otters and pigeons and ball pythons in a white laundry basket and carries the basket to Buck Deco's designated petting zoo area: a small rectangle of dead grass fenced in by wooden stakes and chicken wire. Georgia and Isaiah lift the larger animals together: a snapping turtle; a deer with two tongues; a ten-foot-long pike in a knitted orange sweater and small wire-framed reading glasses, a miniature copy of *The Odyssey* taped to one of its fins.

Ah! Elsie yells. The moths. We mustn't forget the moths.

I'm not wearing a luna moth pinned to my shirt again, Georgia says. It was furry. It made me a pariah.

Elsie opens a small glass case filled with delicate taxidermy butterflies and moths, their wings held in place by round pins. She selects a white moth with black and green spots, its wingspan larger than her palm.

At least in your hair? she asks. Please? You love John Mothefeller.

Georgia grumbles while Elsie sections off her daughter's hair and ties it back. She pins John Mothefeller onto the elastic at the back of Georgia's head like a bow.

Isaiah sits in the grassy pen and pets a stuffed albatross with a rose-coloured beak, a yellow head, and white feathers with black tips. His father has never been keen on having pets, which Isaiah thinks is probably for the best, considering how Arlo would likely treat a cat or dog. Isaiah has always been most jealous of the kids at Bible study whose parents got them birds—blue budgies and green parakeets that hop on their shoulders. When he was eight years old, Isaiah politely asked his father for a little yellow budgie from Minden Pets for Christmas. I'll pay for all its food myself, he stammered. You won't have to d-do anything. I'll take good care of it.

It will sing and scream incessantly, Arlo snapped. Your *gift* will make our lives a living hell.

Isaiah nodded, his gaze shifting to his shoes.

Arlo tilted Isaiah's chin upward so that their eyes met.

Why don't we give gifts in our home, Zi?

Because it's self-absorbed, he said.

Isaiah remembers holding his breath, hoping his answer was good enough to avoid a smack.

That's right, Arlo said, giving his son a gentle pat on the cheek. We gift our time to our community instead.

As Isaiah gets older, his envy of others leads him to lament the childhood he never had. Is it ungrateful to mourn a dream? A version of himself that might've been more confident? Suffered less anguish? Been less sheltered? Less afraid? Isaiah isn't sure. He pets the massive stuffed albatross in the Buck Deco Taxidermy Petting Zoo and allows a childlike fascination to bubble up within him, instead of pushing it down as he normally would. He lets the younger Isaiah in his mind see the glass-eyed bird in all its strange beauty, touch it with his hands, experience pure joy, free from judgment.

The Happening begins when the sun goes down. Tents covered in strings of fairy lights fill the park's soccer field. Each tent is run by someone from town. They sell things like homemade peach soap and hand-poured peach-scented candles and small dolls carved out of peach pits. All the items for sale are things that none of the tourists wanted in the summertime. The people of Port Peter only buy the odd peach-themed artisanal items out of pity for one another. They know how long the winter will last—how far the summer money must stretch. It isn't enough. It is never enough. Nobody runs a booth at the Happening for fun; it is always out of necessity.

The park pathways are lined with hand-held gas lamps from the hardware store so that people can see where they're going as they move from one event to the next. A half-deflated bouncy castle sits at the bottom of the hill, where the Peach King and Peach Queen stand and wave to their subjects. Two game stalls near the porta-potties: a shooting range, and Guess the Duck, where kids use magnetic fishing rods to catch rubber ducks in an inflatable pool, flipping them over to see if they caught the winning duck. There is no winning duck.

The Buck Deco Taxidermy Petting Zoo is a hit every year. It has much better attendance than Rick's Magic Show: sponsored by Royalty Mortgages Ltd. on the mainstage. Rick is seventy-four and wears leggings that show the outline of his balls. He embarrasses kids by voluntelling them to participate in his tricks and blaming them when the tricks don't work. The kids always cry, and Rick ends the show early after shouting profanities.

The food vendors congregate in the parking lot. Blooming onions and bags of caramel corn and pulled-pork poutines and deep-fried peaches on sticks. The Lions Club sells peaches from cans served with scoops of freezer-burnt ice cream.

When Georgia goes back to the taxidermy petting zoo to supervise so her mother can eat dinner, Isaiah returns to the rose garden, where the staff of the Hanged Man pub sell clear plastic cups of watery beer and other drinks. He orders a peach juice and vodka, desperate to get budgies and his father out of his thoughts.

Isaiah has only ever gotten drunk once in his life up to this point: at sleepaway Bible camp. He and Gabriella Vanderhaven shared a box of unblessed communion wine in the woods behind the boys' and girls' cabins on the last night before they were to return home. The two of them had attended the same Bible camp together since they were six. They played Mary and Joseph in the nativity play until they outgrew the costumes.

That night at Bible camp, they drank until the stars blurred together. They stripped down to their underwear and swam in the Minden River. They held a fake river wedding in the dark, giggling and reciting made-up vows and prayers. They did this so that their finale could be the consummation.

Isaiah's head buzzed with alcohol, and he could only stay hard for a minute or so, just enough for a handful of thrusts, and Gabriella could not find a comfortable position to lie in, and they both laughed so hard they couldn't breathe, reeking like lake water and wine.

They were caught by one of the camp counsellors, who promptly told Father Bloom.

If Isaiah thinks about the sequence of events for too long, he starts to feel real physical aches in his body, as if he were punished just hours earlier rather than years. He downs his vodka and peach juice and orders another. If he can't ignore the pain, he will drown it.

<u>Isaiah does not feel the world break</u>

> until he is finished
> his fourth or fifth drink. Too confused
> to tell ashes
> from dust. Abba turns
> wine to water turns time
> to water and the current

carries Isaiah
from the drink line to lying
in a bed

of dead rose bushes, bloody palms
from hardened thorns.
Half-buried

under cool earth. The moon is a cartoon

eye, not quite open
wide, and the firmament

splits,
a rock cracked
by ice. Isaiah—

—tries to get up, but falls forward onto the grass, knocking over a gas lamp. He snickers. The entire scenario is simply too funny. It is too dark. The earth is rotating too fast. He and Georgia ate too much corn dog. Georgia. Where is Georgia?

He manages to get himself to a standing position. His body sways. The ground is water. The earth notices that Isaiah is walking strangely and rotates faster in response. Pain behind his eyes. Bile at the base of his throat. Ground as grass. Ground as boat. Ground as bird.

Isaiah doesn't see the woman in front of him until he bumps into her, tripping and falling back onto the grass. He breaks into laughter.

I'm very *really* sorry, he says, snickering. I know I don't sound like I am but I'm the most sorry I've ever been. Truly.

He cannot see the woman's face properly in the dark. The outline of her body shifts and moves and Isaiah is so, so dizzy.

It's alright, the woman says. Do you need help?

With what specifically? Isaiah asks. There are a lot of things I could need help with.

Help walking. Getting to where you need to go.

Isaiah burps.

I need to go *out*. Out of here. Outta this town.

The ground is water and the waves are rough. Isaiah sways. The woman grabs hold of him to keep him steady. Now, closer to the light of the gas lamp, Isaiah can see her face. Black hair. Age lines.

Sit, she says. On the ground here. I'll get you some water.

Isaiah plops himself down while the woman buys a bottle of water from the nearest food truck. Why would he need water, though? He is surrounded by water on all sides. He is in a boat. He *is* a boat. He himself is the water, spreading out as far as the eye can see in every direction, turbulent and beautiful.

Suddenly, the woman is back, and a bottle is being pressed up to Isaiah's lips. He drinks and lets the water drip down his chin.

This doesn't taste like peaches, he says.

What's your name? the woman asks.

Isaiah Abel Bloom, Isaiah says. That isn't your name too, right? It would be *strange* if we had the same name.

My name is Kind, the woman says.

Isaiah ponders this.

That's *kind* of a cool name, he says.

Thank you, Isaiah. Are you here with your mother?

My mother, Isaiah repeats. Where is my mother?

A pause.

She is coming later, Isaiah says. With my father. Father Bloom. Father *Father*.

Kind nods.

What time will they be here?

A time to dance, Isaiah sings, and a time to die, and a time to reap, and a time to sow—

I need you to do something for me, Isaiah, Kind interrupts. Are you listening?

Isaiah nods so hard that his chin hits his chest.

I need you to tell your mother to go to the cliffside lookout, the one off County Road Five, as soon as she can.

Isaiah tries to make sense of what is happening. But the stars above him seem to melt, dripping down the width of the sky all the way to the ground.

I—he starts, snickering. I don't understand.

You will, Kind says.

Isaiah looks up at Kind, disoriented.

I need to find my Georgia, he says. She is blond. And she wears bright clothes. No shoes. I'm very in love with her.

Kind smiles. It is a warm smile—one that Isaiah recognizes, though he isn't sure where from. Then she looks to her left, as if hearing something. Isaiah cannot hear anything at all. She turns back to him.

I have to go now, she says. Both our families are looking for us, I suspect.

Looking for him? Who? Isaiah cannot remember why he is in the park in the dark in the first place. What *is* he doing here?

Please don't forget about my message for your mother, Kind adds, standing up.

Right. The message. What was the message again?

When Isaiah looks up to thank Kind, she is gone.

He turns his head to each side. People walk along the rose garden paths, their shadows from the gas lamps stretching far in front of their bodies. People laugh and eat and move around him. Isaiah's head pounds with the rhythm of his beating heart. One—two. One—two. One—two.

It takes some time for him to stumble from the rose garden back to the Buck Deco Taxidermy Petting Zoo. How much time? Isaiah's been speeding up and slowing down and stopping and starting again all night.

The chicken-wire fence seems so far in the distance, minutes and miles away, until it isn't, and Georgia Jackson is right in front of Isaiah, the moth still clipped in her blond hair. She grips Isaiah by the shoulders.

Can you even hear me? she says. I've asked you twice already.

Asked what? Something about Georgia's voice is very funny. Isaiah covers his mouth, sputtering, but the laugh escapes his lips anyway.

Georgia's eyes widen.

Oh. Fuck. How much did you drink?

An independent amount, Isaiah slurs. This is me being in-de-pen-*dent*.

Georgia opens her mouth to speak, but a hand appears on her shoulder. Arlo seems to emerge out of nowhere. Out of the dark. He's alone, without Isaiah's mother. The earth rotates faster. Isaiah is nauseous.

Thank goodness, Arlo says. I've been looking for you since I arrived.

Fuck. Fuck. Fuck. How do sober people act? What is a normal thing to say?

Here I am, Isaiah mutters.

He stares down at his shoes. He tries to focus on them so that his eyes don't give him away. How are aglets made? How much do aglets cost, on their own? Why do stars spin so quickly?

Look at me, Arlo says.

Isaiah meets his father's eyes. The moment is so odd—so forced—that Isaiah cannot help but laugh.

Arlo stiffens. Gaze turns to glare. The threat of violence is immediate, and yet, Isaiah cannot stop laughing.

I'll take him home, Georgia says.

Arlo lowers his voice.

You're drunk?

The accusation is hilarious. Isaiah cannot even remember drinking. He would never do that. It is the earth and all its rotating. Yes. That must be it.

We have business to discuss, Isaiah slurs. You. And me.

Isaiah, Arlo starts, his voice no louder than a whisper. There are a lot of people here.

Shh, Isaiah says loudly, his finger to his mouth. It's my turn to talk. My talk. My turn. It's turning into my talk.

Elsie is behind Georgia, now. Even in the dark, Isaiah can tell passersby are watching.

Arlo laughs. He puts his hands in his pants pockets.

This moment feels important to Isaiah—fleeting, more ephemeral than others. If he doesn't say what he needs to now, he may never get another chance.

I want bookshelves, he says.

Bookshelves, Arlo repeats.

That's what I said, Isaiah says. Bookshelves. The extra-tall ones. Just for myself. Nobody else.

He stumbles. Georgia catches him by his arms.

Take him home, Arlo says to Georgia.

I was *not* done, Isaiah whines.

His father leans in close.

Yes, Arlo says through his teeth, you are.

He grips Isaiah's shoulder hard, his fingers digging into the muscle.

But for the first time, Isaiah notices that he and his father are almost the same height. And that observation brings with it a sudden bravery, swelling before he can consider the consequences of his words.

I got into Trinity three times, he says, with scholarships, and part of me kind of wanted to go, I think, because the praying and the reading and the city and the not being around you would be a sweet deal, but every time I got an offer of admission, I'd be like, what kind of Isaiah would I be in seminary, because all of my Isaiah-ness is from getting the shit kicked out of me every day, so if I'm not getting the shit kicked out of me, I'm literally not Isaiah anymore, which would make me no one, which is fucking terrifying, and I also have no idea how to be a good priest because you're the only example I have, like I'm supposed to see God in everyone but I don't know how to do that because I don't think you know how to do that or I hope you don't know how because that would be worse, seeing the God in me but choosing to hurt me anyway, but maybe you just want to hurt God—maybe that's why you kill everyone around you.

The next moment passes before Isaiah can register it. He blinks and Georgia is standing in front of him, a barrier between him and Arlo, and Arlo's hand is raised, but frozen, because Georgia has caught Arlo's wrist in mid-air.

Arlo and Georgia look at one another. Eyes wide and breath held. Isaiah cannot see the looks of disbelief on the faces of passersby, or hear the people of Port Peter laughing in the Buck Deco Taxidermy Petting Zoo. He cannot feel the earth rotate any longer. It is only Arlo, only Isaiah, only Georgia, just the three of them, frozen in time.

Arlo's gaze hardens into a glare, but his eyes water.

What the fuck do you think you're doing?

Georgia lowers Arlo's arm and releases it. The adrenalin of the moment begins to fade, and panic floods Isaiah's body. The earth is back on its rotation, spinning, spinning, spinning, faster, faster, nauseous, embarrassed, terrified.

Georgia is crying. She walks forward until there is no space between her and Arlo.

Hit me, she says.

People are watching now. Port Peter locals who will gossip about this to their neighbours at the laundromat tomorrow morning. It seems inevitable that Isaiah will have to move quickly to put himself between Georgia and harm. Maybe it will be enough. Maybe God will give Isaiah this one thing. This martyrdom.

Please, Georgia whispers.

And just as Isaiah begins to move, Arlo takes a step backward.

You're pathetic, Arlo says.

And he turns and walks away, down the park pathway, until he is completely out of sight.

Georgia?

Yes, Isaiah?

Am I dead?

No. You're in your bed, in the vicarage, in Port Peter. You're very much alive. You're drunk, but you're sobering up. I'm feeding you dinner rolls and giving you water.

Georgia?

Yes?

Are you angry with me?

No, Isaiah.

Okay. You just—you look sad.

I'm not sad.

Oh. You're just thinking?

Just thinking.

Isaiah?

Yes?

Do think you can ever go through life and not hurt anyone at all? Like, actually be harmless?

I don't know. I don't think so.

Georgia?

Yeah?

Mistakes aren't the essence of who you are, though. They're...pages. In a book. A book of you.

What colour book am I?

Bright red.

Georgia?

Yes, Isaiah?

I'd like to read the book of you.

Would you let me read you too?

I would try.

I would read you slowly. If that helps.

It does.

And you would read me slowly too, right? Isaiah?

Yes. Very slowly.

Georgia?
   Yeah?
   Have you ever had a bird inside your head?
   What kind of bird?
   Any kind. Different kinds.
   I don't think so. Do you have one?
   I think I have more than one.

Isaiah?

Yes?

Do you think that the birds in your head will ever go away?

I don't know. Maybe they never go away. Maybe they just get quiet.

Maybe.

I don't know what it's like to have an empty head, though. What if I stop being me?

Isaiah?

Georgia?

I would love you with or without your birds.

How do you know?

It is still night when Isaiah wakes, his head pounding, Georgia curled into him, half her body falling off his twin-sized bed. A half-eaten dinner roll sits on his nightstand beside Georgia's John Mothefeller pin. The vicarage groans in its sleep, wood floors and frame creaking like the sounds from a restless, dreaming child. Isaiah considers going back to sleep. Then he remembers: he hasn't prayed his evening office.

He carefully lifts Georgia's arm off him and steps off the bed onto the floor. He finds his black peacoat downstairs on the kitchen floor. Still half-awake, he swallows two Advil and takes a prayer book and a King James Bible from his father's study.

The night sky is blue and grey. Cloud covered. Isaiah descends the wooden steps from the backyard down to the beach. Wind whips Lake Ligeia into a panic, and her green water sloshes in all directions. High peaks and low valleys.

When he looks around for a place to sit, he notices another person farther down the beach, sitting on a large rock. He walks closer. A head of white-blond curls comes into view. Arlo Bloom, a prayer book in hand. Isaiah walks until he is a foot or so away from his father.

Arlo looks up but doesn't say anything. A lit pillar candle illuminates his small patch of beach. He points to the top of the open page in his prayer book.

Psalm 63—page 405, he says.

Isaiah sits on the rock beside his father and opens his own prayer book. Page 405. Psalm 63.

O God, thou art my God;
/ early will I seek thee.
My soul thirsteth for thee, my flesh also longeth after thee,
/ in a barren and dry land, where no water is.

Thus have I looked upon thee in the sanctuary,
/ that I might behold thy power and glory.
For thy loving-kindness is better than the life itself:
/ my lips shall praise thee.

Arlo reads a verse of the psalm, pausing in silence at each slash for the duration of a *my Lord and my God* before continuing the second half of the verse. Isaiah reads the next verse, pausing in the middle as his father does. The two of them go back and forth—smoothly, and without awkwardness. Two sets of walking legs, perfectly in stride.

They each read one of the two lessons. They pray the Magnificat and the Nunc Dimittis and the Creed and the collects for the day. They finish with the sign of the cross and a moment of quiet. Both exhale.

Feeling better? Arlo asks.

Isaiah nods.

I'm sorry, he says.

He doesn't know what else to say. Shame tightens his throat.

You're forgiven, Arlo says.

You don't have to say that if you don't mean it.

It's what a good priest would do.

He sighs.

Did Georgia help you home?

Yes. She fed me bread.

She didn't walk back home on her own, correct?

She's still sleeping inside.

Not on that dreadful loveseat in the family room.

In my bed.

Good. I'm glad you gave it up for her.

We shared it, Isaiah says.

Arlo takes his hand off Isaiah's shoulder.

We didn't do anything, Isaiah continues. If that's what you're thinking.

Arlo doesn't say anything. He looks out at the lake, his eyes following the dark waves.

I like her, though, Isaiah continues. A lot. We've made plans. Like moving to the city and being roommates and writing together. I asked her if she'd want to do that and I didn't think she'd say yes but she did. I like her a lot. And she likes me. And I think this is the start of something.

Despite Arlo's erratic qualities, Isaiah has often found himself compelled to confess around his father, his innermost life drawn out of him before he can protect it behind a wall of logic. He isn't the only one. Most of Arlo's weekly schedule at St. Andrew's in Minden was filled with back-to-back confessions. Something about him draws out the truth—either a good heart that creates a sense of safety and understanding, or a deeper darkness that might match that of the confessor.

On this night, on this beach, forgiven for the Happening, and hungover from the alcohol, and buzzing with the hum of new love, and flushed with faith and connection from praying the office with his father, Isaiah Abel Bloom can only see his confession as something good. Maybe *he* is good.

Isaiah cannot stop himself from smiling at this realization. And he turns to smile at his father.

But Arlo is still staring out at Lake Ligeia. Still silent.

Isaiah's smile slips.

Dad? Are you okay?

Arlo keeps his gaze forward. He shakes his head. No.

What can I do? Isaiah asks.

Isaiah has no warning before Arlo yanks him upright and throws him forward with so much force that he falls face-first into the shallow lake water.

Isaiah gasps. The freezing water doesn't register as cold at first—only as immense pain. His clothes are soaked through. He usually has more time. Arlo's tells: movements or moods or tones of voice that hint that he is itching for violence. There is no time for Isaiah to take a breath again before Arlo lifts him back up by the scruff of his shirt and pulls his head forward under the water. Isaiah kicks, and the kicks splash the lake water up and out and everywhere, but Arlo holds Isaiah's head still.

After a minute or so, Arlo pulls Isaiah back above the surface. Isaiah coughs a desperate, choking cough, gasping like a washed-up guppy, and again, before he can take a full breath, Arlo yanks him back down under the water.

Isaiah flops and fights and twists but Arlo is stronger. Isaiah is so sweet that Lake Ligeia eats him up and spits him back out and up and out and up and out and it doesn't make sense, it wasn't supposed to be like this, he's not ready, a burning in his chest and nose, his vision blurring the dark of the water and the dark of the sky into one.

He's not ready. His father loves him. His father is good his mother is good Georgia is good Isaiah is good Isaiah is not ready Isaiah can't remember Psalm 23 he knows it he knows that he knows it he can't remember it though I walk through the valley the valley of death the shadow you comfort me your staff comforts me though I walk you comfort me all the days of my life my love I love all the days of my life I love your death your valley you valley me you love the shadow you love death you comfort in the shadow though you comfort me love me you comfort me

please I walk with you in the valley of death it hurts please
is in the shadow is with me is comfort your staff is comfort
the hurt is my life the hurt is your love I can't remember
though I walk I can't remember the valley of death I fear
I remember I'm afraid of remembering please I'm in love
you're afraid I'm not ready I'm not ready I'm all the days
of my life I'm not with you I'm not ready I remember I
forgive you—

THE THIRD PART OF BIRD SUIT

CALLED

FEAST

DECEMBER 1986

Georgia's late grandparents Wade Jackson and Etta Hayes ran a daycare out of their home when Elsie was a kid. Elsie learned to paint in those years. She knelt at the coffee table in the living room and used chalky watercolour pucks and old brushes with split tips to paint surrealist portraits of the other young girls that her parents took care of. The girls in the portraits were always human–animal hybrids. Little billy goat girl. Little muskrat girl. Little heron girl. Elsie understood animals better than she understood children. The portraits were windows into the souls of the girls around her.

Every little animal girl in Elsie's paintings had an expression of deep sadness and unimaginable pain because her models dripped melancholy. The other girls at the home daycare were always sad. Each one arrived crying, screaming for her parents, which was loud sadness, and later, after Wade Jackson brought them into his room for nap time, they floated around like ghosts, with empty eyes and no acknowledgement of the world around them, which was quiet sadness. Elsie understood that quiet sadness. She felt it in her stomach. Wade Jackson made sad girls like a baker made cookies. He made tray after tray. Elsie and the sad girls did not understand this until much later.

As she got older, Elsie found that the sadness was most noticeable when she was alone. So she resolved to never be alone. Never without a boyfriend or lover or one-night stand. She was fifteen when she found out that she was pregnant, the father long gone. Wade and Etta changed the locks to their house and threw her clothes onto the front lawn.

It was the last time Elsie Jackson saw her parents alive. The father of one of the sad girls from the home daycare ran a red light and slammed his Ford F-150 into Wade and Etta's canary-yellow Volkswagen Beetle three years later.

After she was kicked out, Elsie moved in with her childhood babysitter, Arlo Bloom, and his twin sister, Roselyn, who were fourteen years older than her.

The Bloom twins grew up in town, but had been in Toronto for the past two years at school. Roselyn didn't finish her MFA. She said that the craft workshops made her loathe poetry, and loathe poets, and loathe teaching, and loathe writing, and loathe humanity, and loathe herself—though she admitted that the self-loathing started a bit earlier. Arlo graduated with an MDIV and completed his postulancy, but still hadn't been approved for ordination. The two of them decided to move back home while they waited for the approval.

Arlo and Roselyn's father was only home once every couple of weeks. He drove an eighteen-wheeler, delivering crates of peaches over the border in August and Coca-Cola the other eleven months of the year. He had large hands and greying hair and a sincere belief that the moon landing was faked. The twins' mother was somewhere in Australia—they didn't know where exactly. She called once a year, on their birthday, and made a handful of promises that she didn't keep.

Elsie goes into labour halfway through the Christmas Eve midnight mass service at St. Paul's Anglican Church. Her water breaks all over the red prayer bench she's sharing with an older woman during "Away in a Manger." She steps in her own wet, and the lady whispers, Hallelujah, bitch.

Everything halts. The Vicar says that Elsie should not be moved—there isn't enough time to bring her to the hospital. No one argues. Roselyn brings Elsie plastic bottles of water from the daycare downstairs. Arlo removes his winter coat and lays it at Elsie's feet. Each twin holds one of Elsie's hands.

Mother Mary watches from the stained glass above as Elsie gives birth on the floor between two pews. God's gift of life rips her open like a Christmas present.

The baby girl opens her mouth so wide to scream that Elsie thinks she might devour the whole world. She has dark blue eyes like Elsie's. Still, Elsie doesn't understand how she could have made such a creature. She wraps her stranger of a baby in a white tablecloth.

The Vicar knows where Elsie is headed. Everyone in the congregation knows. But they pretend this is a happy occasion. They congratulate Elsie. They bless her new daughter. When it is time for Elsie to walk to the cliffside lookout, they don't stop her. It is a kind of mercy, in its own way.

Elsie tells Arlo and Roselyn to go home—she will meet them there when she has done what she needs to do.

The air is winter dry when Elsie reaches the cliffside. She lies panting against the lookout rocks with the girl in her arms.

The baby shrieks. Elsie isn't sure if she is crying from the cold or crying because she knows what is about to happen. Are babies intuitive like that? she wonders. Shouldn't a mother know what her baby is thinking? This is for the best, then, if there is some motherly intuition that Elsie doesn't have. A bad mother is worse than no mother at all.

The basket is exactly where it is supposed to be when Elsie gets to the cliff's edge. Elsie can hear the water crash against the rock face below. The baby screams and screams. Elsie's hands shake. She looks at the empty basket.

Will the baby die from the cold before anyone arrives? Where will she be taken? What if the baby girl's last thoughts are like those of an abandoned family dog waiting for their loved ones to return? Should Elsie tell the baby what is happening? Would she even understand?

Elsie places the swaddled baby in the plastic basket. Turns to walk away. The baby wails louder than before. Elsie turns and screams back. Hot tears stream down her face.

I don't fucking have what you want, she yells. I don't fucking have it. I don't have fucking anything.

And she turns, and she leaves, back towards the wooded trail, back into town, before she can change her mind.

When Elsie returns to the cliffside the next morning, she can see a tiny body in the bundle of sheets from several feet away, but she is too afraid to get any closer. Certain that the baby must be dead, blue from the cold. She sees the white tablecloth move. Then the shrieking from the night before returns, piercing Elsie's eardrums.

She runs to the basket to confirm, and sure enough, the girl's blue eyes are open, and her skin is flushed pink.

The girl is still alive.

JULY 2002

Port Peter has a military fort called Fort Michigan, still standing from the War of 1812. Tourists often come across it by accident. They walk east along the beach until they reach a chunk of rocky cliffside that blocks their path, and they can either turn around and go back the way they came, or take a set of unsteady steps up a slope above them. They cannot see the fort until they are already at the top.

Most tourists are disappointed when Fort Michigan finally comes into view: four log fences, each about twenty feet long, arranged in a perfect square around a wooden watchtower. The tower has been closed for repairs for thirty-seven years. You can walk around the perimeter of the fort in less than two minutes. Georgia has always thought that it looked like a Lincoln Logs set-up inside of a child's playpen.

Fort Michigan doesn't have a heritage museum because the soldiers stationed there from 1812 to 1814 never fought in a single battle. They came close, once. Townies say that American soldiers stormed the Port Peter beach one August night in 1813, but they never made it up to the fort itself. When dawn broke, fishermen found the American soldiers' bodies in pieces. Ripped blue fabric, soaked red. Musket balls half-buried in the sand. Their arrival was meant to be a surprise, so the Canadian soldiers didn't wake up until the Americans were already dead.

Some of the American soldiers could not be identified. Their bodies could not be sent back home. In a graveyard behind St. Paul's church their remains are buried, beneath a single headstone that reads, *For those who faced the lake and lost. When you pass through the waters, I will be with you.*

Georgia Jackson is forced to attend a Canada Day event at Fort Michigan with her mother and Mark II when she is sixteen. Elsie lays out an old white comforter near the entrance to the fort and sells taxidermy robins and blue jays and cardinals and crows dressed in miniature redcoat uniforms that she sewed herself.

Inside the log walls, Georgia sits on the half-dead grass eating peaches and melted Neapolitan ice cream in a wax-lined paper cup, watching Ryan Frankel and the other War of 1812 re-enactors sweat in their wool redcoats. A local U2 cover band called Elevation performs a few feet away. The lead singer of the band works part-time as Georgia's math teacher.

Halfway through "With or Without You," Mark II joins Georgia on the grass.

That lady was giving me the stink eye, baby girl, he says. I think she thinks you and I are dating.

Right, Georgia says.

He chuckles, gently patting her knee.

You'd be good up there.

Up where?

Over there. In a bonnet and an apron, churning butter.

No thanks.

It would be fun to dress up and pretend we're from a different time.

Fun for you, maybe.

Mark II laughs again, a big boisterous laugh, and Georgia can't help but notice that the dimples in his cheeks look like hers.

You'd have fun, he says. You and I are similar. Don't you think?

Not really.

You know what I mean, Georgia, he says.

And she does, or she thinks she might, though Elsie has never outright said it. She knows that her mother and Mark II first met when Elsie was a teenager and he was on vacation in Port Peter with his college roommates. She knows that they reconnected years later, which led to them dating again. When he passes out on the worn leather couch with the TV still on at full volume, his hand half-buried in a bag of ketchup chips, Georgia sits in the armchair across the living room from him and studies his face, the shape of his chin and the roundness of his cheeks and the slight hook to his narrow nose, and she sees herself, or parts of herself, the parts that she can't stand to look at, the parts that she wants to slice off with a bayonet, and it is clear, then, that he is her father, but it can't be true, it doesn't make sense, because a father would never treat his daughter like a partner or a plaything, and Georgia is not certain that God exists, but if He does, He would not allow something like that.

Mark II places his hand atop Georgia's in the grass and threads his fingers between hers. His weight keeps Georgia's hand pinned down.

Maybe people will be dressing up like us in another two hundred years, he says. I think about that a lot—how those people will remember us. Do you ever think about that?

Georgia nods, heart racing, gaze forward towards the redcoat teens and their muskets. Not everything should be remembered, she thinks.

AUGUST 2019

Georgia watches the woman from up high.

The booth doesn't allow room for movement. Two technicians—one for light and one for sound—sit in old office chairs with peeling leather, hunched over boards of buttons and switches and dials and sliders illuminated red and green like traffic lights.

Sound wears bulky headphones with big foam ear cushions. She adjusts levels and mutes and unmutes wireless microphones. She fades music in and out. Her eyes are cast down, fixed on the Mackie thirty-two-channel console, and she shuts them every so often, listening, watching the performance below as a collection of beats and tones.

Lighting keeps their eyes on the stage but their head perked up slightly, like a dog whose ears rise at the sound of the doorbell. They listen for Georgia.

Georgia kneels on the black booth floor. She watches the stage and gives Lighting verbal cues for the switchboard. Cue twenty-eight. Cue twenty-nine. Brighter on stage left. Cue thirty. Cue thirty-one.

The Essex Hotel in Toronto is a small concert venue, with room for roughly two hundred people in rows of fold-out chairs facing a low stage. No rings of seats above or overhanging balconies. A bar at the back of the Ess that sells six-ounce plastic cups of Greenbelt wine and room-temperature tallboys of Bud Light. No snack concession, but if you tip the bartender well, he'll microwave a bag of popcorn in the staff room down the hall and bring it back for you. Long marks along the walls where peeling sixties-style floral wallpaper has been ripped off. The audience lights have no dimmer, so when the performance starts, patrons are left in complete darkness, fumbling for their drinks and feeling around for their lovers' hands. The seats have no space between them. Knees touch. Drinks left on the ground often spill, giving the space an aroma of old wine and smoke machine glycerin. The bathrooms in the basement are only used by those who don't fear death or the occasional centipede colony. All these things make the space intimate and archaic in equal measure.

The Ess is Georgia's biggest venue to date. It splits its lineup evenly between indie bands and stand-up comedy sets, but each year it keeps enough days in a row open to schedule the winning play in the David Essex Memorial Playwright Competition. This August, that play is *Bird Suit*.

A handful of Georgia's one-acts have won script contests and been featured in fringe festivals across the province, but *Bird Suit* is her first full-length play.

Georgia moved to the city from Port Peter when she was twenty-three. She found a room in an apartment in Scarborough with five other girls—all nursing students at the university. She worked seventy-hour weeks as a convenience store clerk in the Danforth and as a nanny in North York and as an assistant stage-hand at the Princess of Wales Theatre downtown. Her stage-hand job was only two to four hours per week, but she was determined to climb the ranks and make it something bigger. She was close with the box office clerks and the understudies and the makeup artists and the playwrights and the stage managers and the directors. She never sold herself short, they said. She was more electricity than woman. Both light and lightning—useful and dangerous. When she wanted something, she got it, no matter how long it took.

She started thinking through her play ideas while nannying the babies and toddlers of rich North York parents. She would zip them up in plush snowsuits and wrap them in massive scarves like mummies, then stick them in their expensive wagons with sippy cups of organic apple juice and containers of gluten-free Cheerios, pulling them through the city for miles and miles. They occasionally stopped at parks or coffee shops, but they were mostly on the move. All that walking and pulling gave Georgia's mind time to imagine. To construct. To question. To process. To remember.

These walks scared her at first. In the months following her move from Port Peter, she tried to separate and hide her former life in the back of her brain as if they were an elaborate dream. She talked to Elsie on the phone once a week, on Friday mornings, and their rule was that Elsie could not update her on any Port Peter gossip.

Georgia could not admit to herself that she missed Lee at Crime Brûlée, or the smell of paint as her mother painted taxidermy in the house, or her late-night barefoot walks across the boardwalk, Lake Ligeia's warm green water splashing up through the boards and wetting her toes. She could not miss the chicken farm in Ivey, or the peaches and vanilla ice cream at the Happening, or the caves beneath the cliffside. The smell of liturgical incense in Arlo Bloom's car. Felicity Bloom's rosemary bread. Georgia could not let these memories take shape in her mind. She snuffed them out the moment she felt them forming, like putting out the flame of a candle with wet fingers. None of these things could have existed. If they existed, then so did Isaiah.

Isaiah. Laid out in a puddle of water on the kitchen floor. White faced. Blue lipped. Limp. Isn't he cold? Doesn't he need a blanket? Arlo giving him chest compressions. Clothes soaked. Fingers laced. Up and down. Mouth-to-mouth. More chest compressions. No. You're okay. Breathe. You're okay. Again. Again. You need to breathe, Isaiah. Isaiah? That can't be Isaiah. That wet blue thing doesn't look like Isaiah. Isaiah is warm. Isaiah is full of air. Felicity must've called the ambulance. They said they're coming, she says. It is all so confusing. How far is the hospital from Port Peter? How long can the human brain go without oxygen? Arlo pounding his fists against Isaiah's chest. He's sobbing. Please. Breathe. Take me instead. Don't take him. Breathe, Isaiah. Take me. Take me.

Is he pleading with Isaiah, or with God? Can either hear him?

Isaiah Bloom was pronounced dead at the Queen Elizabeth County Hospital at 4:34 a.m. The hospital is in the town of Lakeside—a forty-minute drive from Port Peter. Port Peter has an urgent care clinic, but it isn't a large enough town for its own hospital. The QECH is meant to serve Port Peter, Ivey, and the other towns nearby with less than ten thousand residents.

Port Peter residents call their only ambulance the Hearse because emergency patients often die on their way to Lakeside. They cannot be pronounced dead until they are on hospital property, so there is an odd stretch of time in which the patient is both dead and not dead—a purgatory of sorts.

The elected representative for the area ignores funding requests from the Queen Elizabeth County Hospital. He calls it the quicksand of hospitals. Money goes in, but nothing comes out. He cannot shut down the hospital all at once, because of its necessity, so he simply lets it fall apart, hoping it will one day disappear out of neglect.

The QECH building used to be a public school. The beds double as examination tables. They have paper sheets instead of blankets, and pillows with paper pillowcases. All the beds are in the old gymnasium, separated by clear plastic curtains for the illusion of privacy. The rooms smell clean in a bad way, like fake lemon cleaner and iodine. Like the clean is only there to cover up the terrible things that have happened here.

But the moments following Isaiah Bloom's death were not the moments that hurt the most. The kitchen. The hospital. The funeral. Georgia's grief sat not with the fullness of the bad, but with the fractured quality of the good. It only took a matter of days for the pieces of Isaiah to begin to disappear from her memory. One moment, he was there in her mind's eye: chestnut-brown ringlets and wide eyes and freckles; a gentle, hesitant voice; the smell of frankincense from mass; cream-coloured cardigans; a soft smile into a mug of hot chocolate, steam rising around his face like a fog. Then, suddenly, the picture would be missing something. What did he smell like? Why can't I remember what he smelled like?

It was easier if Toronto Georgia pretended that Isaiah had never existed. What ceased to exist could not be painful. It sat in the body—in muscle aches and joint clicks and nausea, in headaches and fatigue and tension in the jaw—but it did not sit in the brain, where Georgia would have to feel the emotion of it.

Georgia walked and pulled the North York babies in their wagons and fought her own brain for years, refusing to remember. She wrote one-act plays about haunted sex-toy shops and failed art heists and messy divorces between serial-killer duos, and they worked as worthy distractions for a little while.

She did not write about Isaiah until she was twenty-eight. Until the chronic pain in her body prevented her from pulling wagons through the city. Until she confronted a truth: she did not write because she wanted to—she wrote because she needed to. Because if she didn't write about what she'd survived, the anguish of it would eventually kill her anyway.

Bird Suit was born from that need. It follows Isaac, the son of a priest, and Celine, the daughter of a taxidermist, whose memories take the form of birds in their heads. In the script, the birds are externalized, played by real actors surrounding the two principal roles, consistently interjecting reminders of past events.

The young actor playing Isaac is named Devin O'Malley. They are a young nineteen. They often forget their blocking, and they improvise more than Georgia would like. They sometimes have too much caffeine and play Isaac with much higher energy, and they sometimes have too much to drink the night before and play Isaac much more contemplative as they nurse a hangover.

Georgia asked them to audition after watching them as an understudy in a fringe production of *Hamlet*. It has always bothered Georgia that most Hamlets are old, seasoned actors who play the part with poise and precision. Shakespeare's tragic character has always seemed frantic to Georgia—imperfect, near explosion, with a facade of invincibility. A desperation to make adulthood fit right, though its sleeves are always much too long. It is the kind of aura that only someone in early adulthood can have.

The actress playing Celine is Iseul Im. She is still a teenager. She lied at her audition and said she was twenty. Georgia caught the lie immediately, but let her audition anyway. Liars are the best at spotting other liars.

Iseul has had lead roles in several high school plays, but her primary training was at the clown school, where she took workshops on evenings and weekends. Her body acting is incredible, and only getting better. She auditioned for Celine with a scene from *Bird Suit* that had no dialogue. Georgia pays Iseul extra to teach movement workshops for the ensemble of birds in the cast. Iseul's parents have come to every show at the Ess through the week. They always bring her a bouquet of flowers—different kinds and colours each time. White roses. Yellow sunflowers. Mixed bouquets of purple wildflowers. Georgia wonders how Iseul has room in her house for all these flowers, or if she simply throws each bouquet away when the next arrives.

Bird Suit has been on at the Ess for four days now, and tonight is closing night. It is a full house, with patrons packed in every floor seat. The morning after night two, a reviewer at the *Toronto Star* wrote that *Bird Suit* was *bursting with life, not playing pretend so much as reinventing the real. Jackson's first full-length theatre debut dares to voice the question we only ask ourselves alone in the dead of night: How will I be remembered when I'm gone? Don't be caught missing this truly unstoppable show*.

Georgia's eyes are normally on the actors as she calls the lighting cues, particularly the birds, whose fringed costumes are meant to cast feather-like shadows down on the ground and up on the white backdrop.

Tonight, her eyes are on a woman sitting in the front row. Georgia only sees the back of her head at first. A long black peacoat. Dark brown hair pinned up in a French twist, revealing a white clergy collar snug around her neck.

The theatre lights go up at intermission. The priest turns, still sitting, to face another woman in the row behind her, and despite the distance from the booth to the front row, and the distance of eleven years, Georgia can tell with certainty that the priest is Felicity Bloom. Georgia can see a thin chain bordering the woman's clergy collar—at the end of it, a bronze locket. With a little blue bird.

Both women are nodding and talking. Felicity touches the other woman on the arm. Her mouth forms an *O*, then a smile for an *I* sound. Like, Oh, I know, right?

The spotlight above stage left is fucked, Lighting says. I'm fucking with it and it's flickering all fucked-up-like and now it's a fucking horror movie. Fuck me sideways with a flashlight and I'll open my fucking mouth and do a better job.

Sound shifts her headphones so they're hanging over her neck and melts into her office chair, exhaling.

That went okay, right? says Sound. I mean. Better, even. The best first act we've done maybe.

Lighting snorts.

You know those mine-shaft elevators, Kenzie? The ones that shake and take half an hour and take you down to the earth's core or whatever? They stop, eventually. Really far down. And that's where your fucking standards are.

What do you think, Georgia? Kenzie asks.

Georgia watches Felicity stand. The rest of the aisle stands for her, begrudgingly making room for her to walk through. She trails behind the group of patrons racing for the bathroom. She walks until she's out of view, through the theatre doors that lead into the lobby.

Georgia? Kenzie repeats.

I wanna—check something. I'll be quick, Georgia mutters. She rises from her knees and unlatches the booth door. She descends the tall ladder down to the theatre floor.

When Georgia gets to the lobby, the Smart Serve teen manning the concession stand is getting shit from the building manager. Do you think we're *made* of popcorn, Lennox? Do you think we have a popcorn guy who drops off a supply from his popcorn truck out back every morning? This is a goddamn popcorn black market you're running. For fuck's sake.

Georgia scans the lineup for the washroom. The crowd in front of concession. Nothing.

Finally, she sees Felicity at the coat check counter, waiting with a small blue ticket in her hand.

What do you say after eleven years? Something fake? Hi, you look great? She does look great—that wouldn't be fake. More like, You haven't aged a day. More like, Why the fuck are you at my play? Age suits you. Your suit suits you. You're a priest now? You hated praying. And now it's your job. You and your husband are both priests. That's fucked. Or great. Probably both. Where is Arlo? Where's Isaiah? Right. Dead. I remember. You remember too. I remember you. Your rosemary bread and your singing and your fake-flower shampoo and the sounds you made when you touched yourself. You remember me. Whoever the fuck I was then. Whoever I was pretending to be. No shoes. Fucking your husband. Fucking your husband while thinking about you and your bread. And Isaiah. We both remember Isaiah. How's the weather in Port Peter these days? Still the same? Is everything still the same? It fucking better be. It better have stayed exactly the way I left it. I'm sick to my stomach just thinking about it. I'm sick just looking at you waiting for your coat. Do you get to Toronto much? Do you see much theatre? Do you see much theatre about your dead son? Oh my God. Oh my fucking God. You remember me, right? You remember me? *Right?* You remember?

A blaring sound cuts through Georgia's skull. An alarm. The fire alarm. Yelling from the building manager. You left the popcorn in there for *ten minutes?* The smell of smoke and burnt butter substitute. Alright, alright, everybody out. Outside. Everyone.

A woman's voice carries over the loudspeaker. May I have your attention. May I have your attention, please. Our fire alarm has been activated. All patrons are required to leave their seats and exit the theatre in an orderly fashion. The fire department has been called.

Great. On closing night. Georgia can feel the fire alarm in her teeth. In her toenails. Why do they make those things so loud? Why is Felicity Bloom at my play? Let's just burn to death. Death by popcorn. Make it a tragedy. No—a comedy. It would be funny.

It's raining outside on Bloor Street. That hot August rain that rolls off your skin like sweat. No one has their coats. No one has their keys. Like elementary school, a man says, laughing. His wife doesn't laugh. She holds the play's program over her head as if it won't just turn to mush. As if it will protect her despite its fragility. She might as well try. She might as well get a little relief. Even if it is just a little. It is worth it.

The patrons have suit jackets with trendy elbow patches and their best little black dresses with stockings and ruby red heels. Georgia is still in her booth wear—a black T-shirt and black overalls, rolled up to reveal black Doc Martens. A lanyard chandelier of twenty-something keys hanging from her neck. Her natural brown hair tied tight and stuck up into a black beanie. She usually takes the ten minutes between curtain close and the post-show Q & A to scrub down her face and armpits with makeup wipes and change into her midnight-blue blazer, tapered dress pants, and formal Doc Martens—the white ones with less wear that bite deep into her ankle skin.

Twenty-one-year-old Georgia would've hated the outfit, thirty-two-year-old Georgia figures. No sequins. No fur. Shoes. It is strange to Georgia how her younger selves feel like completely different people. Ten-year-old Georgia and sixteen-year-old Georgia and twenty-year-old Georgia. Even twenty-three-year-old Georgia and twenty-seven-year-old Georgia. Even at thirty. At thirty-one. She can only see the changes in hindsight—some small matters of taste; some larger ways of being in the world. She wishes she could gather all the Georgias in one place and show them their similarities. Look, she would say to the teenager. I'm still smoking Benson & Hedges. Hey, Twenty-six: we both sleep with socks on. More comfortable, right? Twenty-eight: the play you're writing right now—the one you're still calling *When Feathers Were the Locks to the Treasure Box*—it's on stage. It's real. You made it real.

But then she'd have to confront all the ways she didn't measure up. The vices. Failed endeavours. Disappointments. Twenty-three: it's ectopic—you bleed every day for a month. Twenty-four: you're using him to distract yourself, and he knows it, and eventually, he leaves you for it. Twenty-seven: you don't get the internship. Thirty: she says yes in front of her family, but pulls you aside after and places the ring back into your palm. How could you put me in that position? she asks. The pomsky puppy gets kennel cough.

He's a Republican. She only stays while you're still drinking, and she leaves when you stop. When the taxi rear-ends the streetcar, a piece of the windshield slices a line through your still-healing *Memento Mori* tattoo. You are devastated. I think it's fitting.

She both pities and envies these Georgias. What they know and what they don't. What they think they know. What they still have, and what they think they'll never get. Who they think they are. What they choose to remember.

And her booth clothes are soaking wet now, and the alarm is still on, and more patrons file out of the theatre into the rain.

A tap on her wet shoulder, harder than a raindrop. And when she turns, it is Felicity Bloom.

Flick, Georgia says.

Peacoat. Crisp clergy collar. Forehead lines. Thin silver hairs at her temples, stark against the chestnut brown. She tilts her little foldable umbrella forward so that it covers the space above Georgia's head. She smiles.

You're wet, Felicity says.

Georgia is suddenly twenty-one again, and twenty-one-year-old Georgia in thirty-two-year-old Georgia's body cannot find words. Any words. So she nods.

Felicity takes a step closer so that the umbrella can cover them both. Her smile slips a little.

It's funny, she says. I thought—well I thought you might not recognize me right away. That you might not remember me.

That wouldn't be very funny, actually, Georgia says. It would be kind of sad.

A pause.

Remembering you is kind of sad too, Georgia thinks.

I'm enjoying *Bird Suit*, Felicity says. So far. The first half. It's very good. The writing. The writing is very good.

I'm sorry, Georgia interrupts.

Georgia isn't sure if she is apologizing for the fire alarm, or for writing a play about Felicity's dead son, or for not inviting Felicity to the play about her dead son, or in condolence for her dead son. Or for looking a little too long at Felicity's lips as she speaks. Perhaps it is all of these things at once.

Felicity nods too hard, for too long. Thinking.

I didn't know. That you wrote plays, or anything else for that matter, until I saw the review in the *Star*. I thought, That's our Georgia, it's got to be. Not ours like we own you, though. We don't. We're not even a we—it's just me, now. In the vicarage. Arlo's... It's just me. You know what I mean.

The fire alarm continues, but it has gone on for so long that its sound is numbing more than piercing. Diluted, like water to wine.

It's, um—Reverend, now? Georgia asks.

Oh, no, Felicity says. He left the Church too. You don't have to call him anything.

I meant you, Georgia says. Do I call you Reverend Bloom?

Felicity shakes her head. Nods. Shakes her head again.

No. Yes, I—people do. The parish does. You aren't people.

I'm not people?

You're Georgia. You're a person. Yes. No, I— You can call me whatever you'd like. I like to be called a lot of things.

I know, Georgia says.

A pause.

I just want to be respectful, she adds.

The corners of Felicity's mouth turn downward a little. Like she's disappointed.

That's very thoughtful of you, she says.

It takes Georgia a moment to realize that the fire alarm has stopped. Patrons are already filing back inside, in from the rain, to watch the second half of the show.

Felicity folds down her umbrella and locks it into place with a click. The warm rain is back on Georgia's hat and face.

Where are you staying? Georgia asks.

I'm driving back home tonight.

Georgia cannot hide her smile. She drives now.

You have to be back for something tomorrow?

They're both wet, now. Felicity's makeup streaks like she's crying.

Not necessarily, she says. Not until Sunday.

It's fun here, Georgia says. Sometimes. It's fun in Kensington, where I live. The neighbourhood has character.

That sounds perfect for you.

Did you already have dinner? I could show you the apartment. And order food. So you can eat before you drive home.

Are you inviting me to your apartment?

Is that weird?

Felicity looks at her shoes.

I could eat. If it isn't an imposition.

It isn't.

Georgia wipes rainwater from her face. She slips her beanie off and shakes it.

I have to get back to the booth for the second half.

I thought you might.

We're having a Q & A after, but then I can meet you in the lobby.

Thank you, Georgia.

It's no problem.

No, Felicity says, taking one of Georgia's hands in both of her own. Really, Georgia. Thank you.

Felicity's hands are cold. Her gesture is so unexpected that Georgia doesn't know what to do. She puts her free hand atop Felicity's hands as if to keep them warm.

You're welcome, Reverend, she says.

Georgia lives in a one-bedroom apartment above a thirty-year-old coffee shop called Sun Bean in Kensington Market. Sun Bean makes the best Americano in the city, and Georgia will fight anyone who says otherwise.

The apartment doesn't have a balcony, but Sun Bean has a small courtyard—enough room for two wobbly picnic tables on uneven ground. Each morning at seven a.m., right when Sun Bean opens, Georgia buys her Americano with room for milk and sits out back in the courtyard and rereads Isaiah's tattered, taped-up copy of *Glass, Irony & God*. The book no longer has a cover. The pages are yellowed and crimped and creased from years of dog-earing. She has been reading it for years, and each time she finishes, she begins again. She reads it slowly, like a type of Lectio Divina—or divine reading—focusing her attention on a stanza, one line, or even one word at a time. She'll chew on the word all day, meditating on it.

Her favourite part of the book is Isaiah's notations, handwritten in pencil throughout. Stars to mark lines he thought were significant. Underlined words that Georgia wouldn't have thought to pay attention to. Short, poignant reactions.

Wow!

True. So true.

Jeremiah 3:18 for sure.

Remembering is a type of prayer?

When Georgia first began to write *Bird Suit*, she found the book in an unopened box of things from Port Peter.

She had forgotten about it—how Isaiah lent it to her in the vicarage on the day they first met. She wept when she saw Isaiah's handwriting. She clutched the book to her chest so tight that the muscles in her arms hurt.

Owning something you were only meant to borrow because the person you borrowed it from is gone is a unique kind of pain. The object becomes both a source of anguish and a kind of talisman. A memory you can hold. A memory that cannot fade. If you can keep this physical object intact for as long as you are alive, you are, in a way, keeping the person alive.

It is just after eleven o'clock when Georgia and Felicity arrive in Kensington, and Sun Bean is closed for the night. Kensington has no street parking left, so Felicity has to park her blue hybrid SUV in the underground parking of a hotel farther down Spadina Avenue. The two women walk back to the Market under a light spittle of rain.

A red door beside Sun Bean opens to a narrow staircase, leading to another, heavier door with three locks, leading to Georgia's apartment. Her space is small, but has high ceilings, which have always made Georgia feel like she's living in a Victorian estate. Bookcases line the walls—some scavenged from people's curbs on moving day, some found at thrift stores. One is sturdy, made of a light oak, and another is black particleboard, half the shelves broken, and another is a metal shelf meant for tools in a garage. Books line every single shelf. Some stacked, some stuffed in whatever free space is left.

Georgia has a pink Edwardian-era chesterfield that the Princess of Wales Theatre had thrown away after the end of a show's run. She has a little wrought iron patio table with two matching patio chairs. Like a French cafe, Georgia has always thought. The hardwood floor bears deep gashes. Only one window in the apartment opens. Every time Georgia boils water to make tea, the steam sets off the fire alarm.

Felicity's eyes eat up the space, but widen when a chirping sound fills the air, followed by the clang of metal.

Sorry, Georgia says, slipping off her coat. That's just Cheerio.

Cheerio?

My budgie. He gets angry when I come home and take too long to say hi to him. He's sensitive like that.

Georgia takes Felicity's coat and hangs it on a hook on her thin coat rack. The chirping is louder now. More clanging.

Yeah, yeah! Georgia yells out. The Duke of Kensington can't be kept waiting.

A redwood china cabinet sits against the wall closest to the couch. The cabinet is really two separate parts, one set atop the other. The top section has two glass doors of equal size that open onto shelf space, where Georgia keeps her knick-knacks. Cheerio's birdcage fits perfectly beneath the top section, supported by the desk underneath.

Georgia removes the hook and spring that keep the birdcage closed. She puts her hand out, palm up, and a little bird with egg yolk–yellow feathers hops out of the cage and up her arm until it is standing on Georgia's shoulder. Chirp chirp. Chirp chirp chirp.

Oh yes, sweet prince, Georgia muses, I know. It's a hard life. Oh how I abuse you. With your baths under the kitchen sink tap and your fresh organic vegetables that are nicer than what I eat and your hourly cuddles and your freedom to fly about that you often exploit to peck holes in our couch.

She walks back over to Felicity, who is still standing by the coat rack. Felicity's brown eyes move from bookcase to bookcase like a pendulum, and as Georgia gets closer, she can see that Felicity is crying, silently, not a hint of pain on her placid face. Felicity turns her focus to Georgia after another chirp from Cheerio, who is tugging at a lock of Georgia's brown hair.

Georgia and Felicity eat smash burgers with shiny buns, dripping with grease. They drink chocolate milkshakes and split a poutine with two forks. They eat until they're stuffed, and Georgia has the urge to unbutton her jeans and splay out on her hardwood floor like she's making a snow angel, but she remembers that Felicity is forty-eight, and a priest, and Georgia is thirty-two, with her own apartment, and lying on the ground seems like something that would've made sense back then, back when they were both young small-town women with nothing to prove, but it wouldn't make sense now. Georgia at twenty-one had no shame. At least, she acted like she didn't. Georgia at thirty-two sweats shame in buckets. She wakes up in the middle of the night, drenched in it, panting.

While Georgia makes pour-over coffee, Felicity fiddles with the gold clasp that keeps her clergy collar in place from the back. A quiet click, and the collar opens like a handcuff. She pulls it from her black turtleneck and sets it on the table in front of her. It holds its round shape. She exhales, slumping back into her chair. Like taking off your bra after a long day, Georgia thinks. She sets the coffees down.

Can I ask you something? Georgia asks.

You can ask me anything, Felicity says. If you give me the same courtesy.

What happened with Arlo?

He left me. Not long after you left town.

Felicity pauses.

Were you in love with Isaiah?

I don't know, Georgia says. Maybe. Where's Arlo now?

In a booth along the boardwalk mostly. He's an exorcist for hire.

Georgia waits for Felicity to smile or laugh—any indication that she's joking. But her face stays slack.

Like, The power of Christ compels you?

I wouldn't know. I've never required his services. When Arlo asked you to join us, what made you say yes?

You, Georgia says. Why did you become a priest?

St. Paul's offered to pay for seminary. I had no money. They had no priest.

Another pause.

And I missed praying with Isaiah, she adds. And I think— I think I was always supposed to be one.

She clears her throat.

Have you dated many people? Since you left?

Four, Georgia says. I was almost engaged once. Do you like being a priest?

I don't think it's about liking it, Felicity says.

Then what's it about?

Answering a phone when it rings. In a sense.

Georgia doesn't understand.

The person you were almost engaged to, Felicity says. Were you in love with them?

No, Georgia says. Why do you keep asking me about love?

Because who we've loved is...a history of who we are. And I want to know who you've been the last eleven years.

You're lying. Your face gets red when you lie.

Felicity stands, her hands on her cheeks.

Why did you come to my play, *Reverend*? Georgia asks.

I should just drive back. I've taken enough of your time.

Is that what you want?

Felicity sighs. She picks up her clergy collar from the table and wraps it back around her neck. She struggles with the gold clasp on the back. Fuck. Come on.

Do you want help?

I want...

And her voice trails off. She grunts in annoyance, trying to pin the collar back.

And Georgia finally understands.

She walks to where Felicity is standing, and she brings her hands to Felicity's neck, around the clergy collar.

Felicity brings her own hands down. Georgia takes the collar off her and places it back onto the kitchen table.

The first time we met, you prayed for me. Do you remember that?

Yes, Felicity says.

You asked God to help me do the things that feel good, Georgia says.

Their faces are close, now. Their eyes locked.

And what would feel good right now, Georgia?

Georgia tilts Felicity's chin up gently with her hand, and kisses her.

The reverend tastes like cheese curd and chocolate milkshake. It is the first time Georgia has ever kissed Felicity. It is less confident of a kiss than she would've given at twenty-one—hard, yet holding back—but Georgia isn't twenty-one. Not anymore.

The moment isn't like Georgia dreamt it would be. A light. A god. An epiphany of some kind. The kiss isn't an idea. It isn't the Divine. It is real. Present. Here on earth, where it is ephemeral and very, very human. But Felicity is right—it does feel good.

Felicity takes Georgia's face in both her hands and kisses her much harder. She backs Georgia up to the edge of the kitchen table. Georgia's hand slips into Felicity's dark hair and the women devour one another.

Suddenly, between kisses, Georgia starts laughing and cannot stop.

What is it? Felicity asks.

You have gravy on your shirt, Georgia says. And I smell like the sound booth. And we've both been rained on.

How large is your shower?

Georgia leads Felicity to the bathroom. The room is so small that the door cannot open completely without hitting the side of the toilet. The mirror above the sink is painted with dried shower spittle. There are dark rings on the counter by the sink where Georgia has left her coffee cups while getting ready in the morning. One bath towel—dark grey, hanging on the back of the door. A smaller white towel on the floor, used as a bath mat. The bathtub is off-white. Porcelain. Rectangular. Half-empty shampoo bottles and tiny hotel body washes and a pink loofah that looks as though it is one scrub away from completely unravelling. There are strands of long brown hair stuck to the tile wall. The shower head is the only thing that Georgia replaced when she arrived. It is wide like a dinner plate, and shoots out enough water to mimic the experience of standing beneath a waterfall.

The shower turns on with a gurgle. It doesn't take long for the water to get hot, for the tiny room to fill with steam.

You get in first, Felicity says quietly, unbuttoning her shirt.

Georgia peels off her clothes and pulls the elastic from her hair. She steps into the tub and turns up the heat until the water burns her scalp and skin a little. Two whole minutes pass before the shower curtain crinkles back and Felicity steps into the tub to join her.

Silence follows. Georgia under the flow of the water, drenched. Felicity in front of her, fully dry. Georgia's eyes fixed on Felicity's arms and shoulders.

I'm sorry, Felicity says. For not saying anything about—I don't know what to call it exactly. My condition.

Felicity is mostly skin, rolls and stretch marks and wiry hair and freckles, but there are patches of Merlot-red feathers along her forearms, her shoulders, her elbows. They don't spread above her collarbones or below her thighs. There are hundreds of them, Georgia thinks. Small like pinky fingernails. Sticking out where bare skin would be.

They started appearing a few months after we moved to Port Peter, Felicity continues. I've tried plucking them out. With tweezers, one by one. It's very painful and they just... grow back, for ten or so years now. A doctor wouldn't know what to do, I think, with this. I thought it might be punishment. Retribution.

Why would you need to be punished?

The condensation from the shower gives Felicity's little feathers a metallic sheen. They almost look like scales.

God knows that I'm not a good person, Georgia.

Georgia reaches out and gently runs her hand down Felicity's feathered arm. It is soft. It is like petting Cheerio, her budgie.

And He loves you anyway, she says, hesitantly, not quite believing her own words.

Felicity kisses Georgia in response. Softly. Her head under

the flow of the shower head now. The red feathers are slick and smooth when they're wet. Georgia admires them, and kisses Felicity back.

Later, when they are both in her IKEA four-poster bed, Georgia lies awake while Felicity sleeps. She spends hours staring at the shadows on the ceiling of her bedroom.

The insomnia isn't new. It started shortly after Isaiah's funeral. She's found ways to cope with it over the years. Melatonin. Prescription sleep medication. Warm milk before bed. Avoiding milk before bed. Trying to imagine the future she wants. Trying to imagine sheep running through a field. Trying to imagine a black hole in outer space, void of anything but itself. She will try anything once.

I just wanted to say fuck You, she whispers to the ceiling. For Isaiah Bloom. He loved You so much. You know that, right? And he loved people. He wasn't one of those fucks who love You and then use that love to scream death threats at abortion clinic nurses. He ripped his whole heart out of his chest and offered it to everyone he met. He didn't deserve to drown. He was going to be a famous poet. He was. I could tell. And now he's fucking nothing. And he didn't do anything to warrant what You did to him. It wasn't his fault. He didn't ask to be treated like shit and then die. It's Your fault. You killed him.

A lump forms in her throat.

I didn't get enough of him. I know that's fucking selfish. I don't know how not to be selfish.

She waits to hear something. To feel something other than anger—a presence or a sense of calm.

It wasn't my fault, she says. The Birds or my mom or Isaiah. Or my father. I didn't deserve that. I was a kid. It's not my fault. You were supposed to protect me and You didn't. You're supposed to love me and You don't. I love You. You're supposed to love me.

Georgia covers her mouth to muffle a sob. The tears are hot on her cheeks.

How can You let all this happen?

JANUARY 2004

The stolen book in Isaiah's coat pocket is clearly visible, but James keeps quiet when he sees it. Since Felicity and Arlo's wedding sixteen years prior, James's calls to his daughter have gone unanswered. Arlo's doing—James is certain. The priest acts like he's kind, but in truth, he's a walking tower of lies: any confrontation and he will topple, falsehood after falsehood, and you will be the one to blame.

When James heard that Felicity's child was a boy, he feared that she might have given birth to a second Arlo Bloom, building him up through childhood as a parallel tower, block after block, lie after lie. How do you raise someone created to be used against you? But when he sees Isaiah Bloom standing in the doorway—eyes downcast, shy, with Felicity's dark curls and dark eyes—James lets out an audible exhale. The boy has Arlo's freckles, but otherwise, there isn't a trace of his father to be found.

James invites the two of them inside. With Isaiah in the library, he leads Arlo into the kitchen to talk. He offers Arlo whisky, which Arlo declines, so he makes coffee on the stovetop instead. Arlo taps his foot compulsively and glances around as if the roof might cave in. Then, he breaks the silence.

Felicity is not like us, he says.

James says nothing.

She needs—something, Arlo continues. I've spent years trying to figure out what it is. But I'm certain that it's something I don't have.

And you're here to find out what it is? James asks.

No, Arlo says. I'm here because I'm going to file for divorce.

Arlo doesn't make eye contact. He stares into his mug of coffee, his face reddening.

Laughter. James cannot not help it. He cannot hold it in. There isn't anything good in you, is there? James asks.

I came to you because I want to ensure that she has support, Arlo hisses. That she is not left with nothing and no one. Because that is the honourable thing to do.

James laughs again, baffled. There are two people sitting in front of him: the man Arlo Bloom *thinks* he is, and the man he *really* is. How do these two men stay so separate from one another? How does a lie become so lifelike—so real?

What about the boy? James asks.

She can see him whenever she'd like, Arlo says. Within reason.

Is that what he would choose?

It's not Isaiah's choice to make.

And all of this makes you *honourable*, James says.

Felicity didn't grow up with her mother, Arlo says. You made that choice for her.

It was the wrong choice, James says. Do you love your wife?

Why would you ask me that?

Because I want to hear you say it.

I'm leaving her *because* I love her, Arlo says.

She won't feel loved.

You mean that she won't feel *happy*. Love isn't always happy.

What is it, then? If not happy?

Necessary.

Is that what you were taught? James asks. Is that the only kind of love you know?

Arlo's eyes fall to his coffee mug. He pushes back his chair.

Isaiah and I should get going, he says.

We don't need to pass down bad love like a family heirloom, James says softly. From father to son to son to son. There's no value left in it. Every time you are loved, you get to choose whether you will pass that same love to someone else. I didn't need the kind of love my father gave me. The kind of fear and shame. I left it behind. And I made a new kind of love. A love of patience. The kind that I craved when I was small. I crafted it carefully out of the few and finite comforting memories I have of my father, and this new love, this is what I gave to Felicity. It isn't a perfect love, but it is better than what I got, and she gets to decide what parts of it she will give to Isaiah, and what parts she will leave behind. And Isaiah will never have to see that original, painful love.

Arlo doesn't respond. He lets silence swallow the room. James sees something, then. A flicker of humanity perhaps. Regret. The anguish of memory. Whatever it is, it makes James feel like his words might have broken through the priest's shell of a body. That maybe, Arlo Bloom isn't the devil incarnate, but just another broken man. Broken men make mistakes. Broken men love the only way they know how.

And Arlo blinks. He turns his head upward so that he's looking James right in the eye. His face a shade of dark red. And James can't see the flicker of humanity anymore. He can't see anything at all.

Some of us deserve painful love, Arlo says.

He rises from his seat immediately, and fumbles with his coat as he walks back down the hall. Calls for Isaiah to come out from the library.

James sees it, then—the book-shaped bulge in Isaiah's jacket pocket. He looks at the boy and the boy looks back at him, frightened, with his mother's eyes.

James remembers the tool shed, with his own books. His only safe place.

And he doesn't say a word.

When Isaiah and his father are halfway down the driveway, their coats and hats flecked with white snowflakes, James watches from the doorway, silent, until Arlo turns back to face him.

You kill everyone around you, James says.

AUGUST 1981

The cliffside children grow up on Kind Farms. When Kind purchases the property, she cleans out the massive barn, removing the hay and mud and rusted tools and aged barrels of tractor oil. She nails tufts of insulation resembling dog hair between the old pine support beams. She hires Port Peter's only electrician and only heating and gas company and only central air company to make the barn livable the whole year round. Then she builds bunk beds in the lofts—ten, then twenty.

The Birds took the cliffside babies and brought them back home under Lake Ligeia at first. They raised them there in the great wide meadow and the sunken ships. It didn't matter who their mothers were: part-time swim instructors or high school dropouts or piano prodigies with full scholarships waiting for them in the city. It didn't matter what the babies looked like or how much they cried or how well they slept. The Birds loved them all, each one for a different reason. They loved one baby's upturned nose and another's long birthmark and another's ankle rolls that made him look like a human croissant. This one yawns like a jaguar, they'd say. This one's looking at me like she can see my entire life, beginning to end.

The babies grew into children, and the Birds taught the children how to do all the things that the Birds knew how to do. Fencing stances. Physics equations. Latin translation. Woodwork. Clarinet. Prose poetry.

But the skilled young children became agitated older children. They were restless, longing for the air in which they were born. They didn't know it, but they craved connection with their own kind.

Kind was the first Bird to propose purchasing the farm. She volunteered to run it herself, coordinating everything that the children would need. She decided which older Birds would run the business side of things. She fought for those children relentlessly until the other Birds finally agreed to let her have her way. Kind cared about them, she really did—though secretly, selfishly, she thought that a farm of Birds in town might help her lost daughter find her way back home. Like a lighthouse beacon.

AUGUST 2019

Georgia and Felicity stop at the Greenbelt ONroute on their way back to Port Peter. It's just off Highway 24, ten minutes before the border crossing into Lewiston, New York.

The women live isolated and blissful in Georgia's Kensington apartment from Thursday night through to six o'clock Sunday morning. It is a short-lived existence of endless Sun Bean coffees and cheap wine and fresh cheese from the specialty shop farther into the market. Felicity buys butter and flour from the grocer down the street and makes Georgia a variety of scones each day, cheddar with chives and white chocolate with cranberry and strawberries with condensed milk.

They drink their coffee and eat their scones together at the table each morning, but they don't engage in conversation. Georgia edits drafts of a new script while Felicity prays her morning office from a small edition of the *Book of Common Prayer* she keeps in her purse. It is the physical closeness—the ability to engage in their art and worship separately while still being near enough to reach out and touch one another—that feels most intimate to Georgia. Even more intimate than the sex, because it is less like pleasure that begins and ends within a certain time frame and repeats itself, and more like pleasure that is ongoing, perpetual, interrupted only by scones and sleep. Felicity takes her in the shower and on the bed, on the pink Edwardian couch and the kitchen counter, on the floor in the entryway and standing with her stomach pressed against the apartment front door, Georgia's eye level with the peephole to the hallway as Felicity fucks her, each thrust forward banging the door to a holy rhythm.

On Saturday night, Felicity is sitting at the table when she asks Georgia to come back to Port Peter with her the next morning.

You don't have to work until next Thursday, right? I could drive you back Wednesday night.

You can't just stay here? Georgia asks.

Guest celebrants are hard to come by these days, Felicity says. You can stay at the vicarage with me. It's nicer now. Art on the walls. Some character.

A pause. Felicity looks up.

You don't want to visit home? she asks.

Toronto is home, Georgia says.

Felicity shrugs. Georgia sighs.

Only to see you preach, Georgia says finally. And to visit Lee at Crime Brûlée.

That dessert shop? Felicity asks. That's been closed for years. It's a bank now.

Felicity continues her writing, but Georgia focuses her attention on a bare section of wall above Felicity's head, trying to fill blank space in her mind where her old life used to be. Confused as to how a landscape she knew so well could ever change without her permission. Port Peter was the kind of town that would absorb you if you let it—like you couldn't tell where the town ended and where you began. Like when you left, or when it changed, or when you changed, there was a kind of betrayal present. Like your foot left your body, walking off on its own, but the hand never gave it permission, and now it must rethink its entire relationship to the body. Where did you go? the hand cries out. Why have you forsaken me?

The Highway 24 ONroute has a Tim Hortons and a gift shop with Canadian-flag shot glasses and stuffed moose in Mountie uniforms and keychains that say *IN ALL THY SONS COMMAND*. There's a gas station that used to sell gas but now just sells cigarettes and chocolate bars and blue raspberry slushies, and gives out the key to the washroom attached to a wooden ruler. Everyone who has ever used the ONroute gas station washroom has done so out of desperation.

The inside of the ONroute is aggressively air-conditioned. Green tiled floors and a roof with wooden beams, meant to look like a cabin. A fountain with fake rocks in the centre of the building, throwing water up into the air in spurts instead of a consistent stream. The fountain is full of kids and their hands are full of pennies, thrown into the fountain like a wishing well. The kids wade through the dirty fountain water and scoop up the pennies. The pennies were once used as real currency, and now they are only used in the exchange of wishes. The kids leave the fountain with soaking jeans and ringworm and pockets full of other people's wishes—wishes that they cannot fulfill. The pennies are only worth the memory they hold. Of a hot August morning in an ONroute. Years from now, when the kids look at the pennies, they will think of this day. They will remember.

Georgia watches the kids and wonders if God is trapped in the same predicament. Weighed down with prayers that He can't answer—prayers that He carries around because they remind Him of us. Prayers that help Him remember.

The drive into Port Peter is unfamiliar. Georgia rarely

left home as a child, but when she did, her return would always be marked by the wide-open peach orchards, acres of them between the town of Ivey and the Port Peter township sign. Now there is no farmland. Instead, there are new condominium complexes and suburban housing developments. A Walmart and a Starbucks and a four-star steak grill. Paved roads and parking lots. A once clear skyline is now an overcrowded painting of recently built apartment buildings and retirement homes. So many new houses that Georgia cannot see Lake Ligeia from the highway without craning her neck, and even then, it is a short glimpse of green between high-rises.

What's all this? Georgia asks.

Felicity takes a sip of her Sun Bean coffee, leaving the car on cruise control.

New families from the city, she says. And retired tourists, too tired to leave after every summer. Businessmen who work just over the border. Money to be made building in the Greenbelt.

There's no way anyone who grew up in town can afford one of these places, Georgia says.

I don't think any of this is for them, Felicity says.

In town, Georgia sticks her head out the car window to get a better look at the new storefronts. A paint-your-own ceramics shop and a mommy-and-me handmade baby clothes store and a Bird-themed breakfast cafe called The Nest. Boutique shoe shops and organic grocers and a second, larger Starbucks. No more payday loan company or Goodwill thrift. No used bookstore.

She thinks she has seen as much as her heart can take until they get to the strip, where Elsie's old taxidermy shop, Buck Deco, has been turned into a Little Caesars.

The only familiar landmark Georgia finds is Kyle's Variety, still kicking near the entrance to the boardwalk. Thank fuck, she thinks.

She gets Felicity to drop her off there. She'll walk around and eat and scoff at the hipsters while Felicity celebrates the nine a.m. low mass. She tells Felicity she'll be at St. Paul's for the eleven a.m. mass.

An overlay of Georgia's memory covers her vision of the Port Peter she stands in. Lanky kids chewing popsicle sticks and spitting the wood splinters onto the boardwalk, walking barefoot through the grocery store parking lot and washing tar off their feet in Lake Ligeia. Women with chunky highlights and plastic sunglasses and rhinestone nose studs buying expired sunscreen from Kyle's for $14.99. The teenaged pub servers sweating buckets in their black cotton shirts, offering half-assed How are yous to the city boys. Thirsty, they reply.

The strip is clean beneath that dirty sheen of memory. The sidewalk cement has been torn up and repoured a bright, chalky white, and there are garbage cans with recycling sections and bins for your cigarette butts. When Georgia walks up to Kyle's Variety, there is no light coming through the windows. She tries the door. Locked. Then, she notices the handwritten sign fixed to the door with painter's tape: *CLOSED INDEFINITELY*.

When Georgia gets to the boardwalk, a metal railing is fixed to its entire length. Metal signs along the rail that read *CLOSED FOR SWIMMING. LAW BREAKERS WILL BE PROSECUTED*. Lake Ligeia's water is more brown than green—swamp-like under the August sun.

Georgia can still see tourist-shop kiosks and stalls and tents and shipping containers along the other side of the boardwalk, but there are fewer than she remembers. One custom T-shirt shop. One freelance massage therapist. A woman selling oddly shaped cotton candy that she clarifies isn't safe for consumption.

The sun feels hotter, like it knows she's no longer a local, just a tourist, and it doesn't mind sending her back to her fancy little city with a satisfying burn. Can you be a tourist in the place you were born?

One tent stands out amongst the rest. It is almost at the boardwalk's end. Big as a backyard shed, with a blue tarp tied down atop thick purple fabric. A young woman with long ginger hair and bangs stands in front of the tent in jean shorts, white sneakers, and a black V-neck tee that reads *EX-POSSESSED*. Georgia gets closer and realizes that the woman cannot be older than nineteen or twenty. There's a small velvet bag around her neck at the end of a long silver chain. A plastic lawn chair to her right. A sign, propped up on the chair:

FATHER ARLO BLOOM

EXORCIST

He has a deal on right now, the young woman says to Georgia, wiping sweat from her forehead with her shirt. It's called the Damned Family Deluxe. You're basically ensuring that the demons he exorcises out of you don't just, like, jump into someone else in your house. That can happen.

Georgia looks over at the woman. She squints from the sun.

What's that around your neck?

Salt, the woman says. For salt circles. We sell that too.

You work for Arlo?

For Father Bloom.

Right. Is he around?

By appointment. You can pay for a consultation.

I'm an old friend of his.

I really can't give people special treatment, the woman says. He gets a lot of business.

Can you tell him I'm here, at least?

He doesn't like to be disturbed while he's making the holy water perfume rollers. Unless it's for a consultation.

How much is a consultation?

One hundred and fifty. Cash only.

That's a joke, right?

Possession isn't a joke, no.

Georgia takes a wad of twenties in her purse from her *Bird Suit* ticket sales and places them in the woman's palm.

I'd like to see him. Now. Please tell him it's urgent.

Absolutely, the woman says. I'll go let him know. If you need me in the meantime, just holler for Kit.

She disappears into the tent, leaving Georgia out in the heat. Thirteen minutes pass by before Kit returns, giggling, straightening up when she sees Georgia.

He's, uh—I mean, Father Bloom is ready for you now.

The fabric of the tent is old-curtain heavy, and it takes strength for Georgia to peel it back and step inside, where the otherwise dark space is illuminated by plastic battery-operated tea lights.

The tent smells like liturgical incense, but too strongly, as if it's being pumped from a smoke machine.

Two long fold-out tables sit in the tent's first section, covered in crucifixes of different sizes, price stickers stuck to each one. Children's dollar-store water guns labelled *HOLY WATER WEAPONS*, and little velvet bags that Georgia can only assume are filled with more salt. There is another cur-

233

tain at the end of the tent's makeshift foyer, drawn shut. Georgia reaches for the rope keeping the curtain closed, but pauses. She looks up.

Don't let me regret this, she whispers. Please.

When she opens the curtain, Arlo Bloom is sitting in a plastic lawn chair, leaning his elbows on a wooden crate covered by dark crimson fabric. He's in what sort of resembles clerical clothing—a white clergy collar affixed to a red short-sleeved Hawaiian-style button-up. His hair is more white than blond. Curls frizzed, with less shape. Age has taken to his face like a plow to a field.

Georgia and Arlo lock eyes. She stays standing. Says nothing. Arlo smirks, and he reaches down to his left and picks up a bottle of Merlot. He takes a sip right from the bottle, then takes a pause, as if considering its quality.

You're here, he says, eyes up from the bottle.

Georgia nods.

Arlo extends a hand towards the second lawn chair, motioning for Georgia to sit. She does. The smell of the wine is overwhelming.

A minute of silence goes by until Georgia clears her throat.

Exorcisms, huh?

Arlo laughs, a little too loud for a little too long. His face is flushed. He takes another sip of wine, more of a swig this time.

Is this an intervention? Or are you in need of my services?

The same services you gave Kit? Georgia asks.

You've met, he says. I'm glad. She reminds me a little of you, in a different life.

She charged me a hundred and fifty dollars to see you.

We all need to make a living somehow, he says. Some of us do it *earnestly*.

This? Is earnest?

I'm selling an experience, he says. I read that review in the *Star*. You're selling stolen goods.

What did I steal?

A story that isn't yours to sell.

Georgia feels heat rise to her cheeks.

Oh dear, Arlo says, chuckling. Did you expect something else when you sought me out? Congratulations on your success Georgia, I'm so fucking proud of you Georgia, Isaiah would be so—

He trails off, nodding. Thinking.

What happened with Felicity? Georgia asks.

I do believe our session's time has run out, Arlo says.

Georgia reaches into her wallet and puts down a toonie.

I already have that one, he says. But thank you.

How soon after the funeral did you abandon her?

That's a strong word.

What would you call it?

Divorce. Quite popular these days. Very modern.

How pastoral of you.

How is Flick these days? Arlo asks. Or did you just come back to see me?

She's great, Georgia snaps.

Arlo laughs again.

You and her. That doesn't surprise me.

I'd like my hundred and fifty dollars back, Georgia says.

That was for a consultation. We consulted.

You're drunk and this is asinine.

Kit and I are having a baby.

Georgia looks at him, for real this time. Convinced that she is dreaming.

That kid out there, she whispers, is having your kid?

I don't need your judgment.

But you need my money.

Arlo whips the bottle of Merlot at the wooden dresser on the far side of the tent. Georgia flinches.

Kit, Arlo bellows.

Kit enters the tent a moment after, standing upright, like a dog ready for an order.

Did you drop something, Reverend?

He gestures at Georgia.

This is the famous Georgia Jackson, he says. The one from the city whose writing you're always going on about.

Kit's eyes light up.

Oh my *God*, she says. I mean, gosh. Ms. Jackson. I didn't recognize you—in your headshot your hair is curled and down, and right now it's straight and up, and you're obviously not wearing that red jacket from the photo. I saw *The Leopolds* at the Hamilton Fringe Festival a few years ago. Twice, actually, and I was like, I bet that one'll win Best of Fringe, and then it did. I'm *dying*, like, absolutely *dying* to see *Bird Suit*. I heard it's about you growing up in Port Peter. That's so original. It's just *so* Georgia Jackson. You really have an identifiable style. A real *you*-ness. I cut out the article and—

Ms. Jackson is a very busy woman, Kit, Arlo says. She has to get going. But I've decided to let her have this session for free. You can give her back her hundred and fifty-two dollars.

Keep the toonie, Georgia mutters.

Of course, Kit says. The float case is just out here, Ms. Jackson. I can get you all settled and whatever else you need—

Arlo glares at Kit.

Right, she says. You can come back outside with me. Thank you for visiting.

Back outside, Georgia tells Kit to keep the money.

I heard you're, um, growing your family, Georgia says. You'll need it.

You're so kind, she says. You're a hero of mine. I hope that's not weird.

I'm not a hero, Georgia says quietly. But thank you. That's really sweet of you to say.

Kit's face lights up suddenly, and she reaches into a bag slung across her chest. She pulls out two printed sheets of paper with QR codes on them. Each says *ENTRY ONE*.

I'm singing at the Grande Arabella tonight, she says. You know that restaurant that's a boat? It's a good gig. I just sing old jazz tunes in the dining room and I get to keep all the tips. Plus Father Bloom and I get free dinner. Anyway. They always give me extra vouchers to bring people along, and I have two here, and you can have them. You could come see me sing tonight, and bring someone with you, and the two of you could have dinner. If you want.

Georgia hesitates, her hand frozen mid-air. She exhales. Takes the tickets from Kit's hand.

That would be amazing, she says. Thank you, Kit.

As Georgia walks back down the boardwalk, she thinks about the baby—Arlo's second chance, in a sense. It could've been with me, she realizes. Easily. She and Arlo slept together once a week for months, unprotected.

Georgia begins to feel something that she desperately tries to shove deep down, away from her awareness. It is a shameful feeling. One that doesn't quite make sense. Envy.

She imagines herself at twenty-one, cradling a budding baby bump. In your beginning was a woman, she would tell her stomach. And the woman was with God, and the woman was God, in a way. A creator of people. A creator of beginnings. This is your beginning, but you are not here. Not yet. This is the starting point. The before that eventually becomes your now. It is a shell. It is a woman. A God. A girl who will never be a playwright. A lover who will one day be your mother.

Georgia is late to the eleven a.m mass at St. Paul's. The parking lot is filled with cars, but she is the only person outside. She half walks, half runs to the front steps, stopping when she notices a large rainbow flag affixed to the overhang above the door. It isn't something she's ever seen at a church before.

Inside, the parishioners who fill the pews are not the same sort that Georgia remembers. They are much younger, with ripped jean jackets and purple hair and earrings shaped like paper clips. A parishioner in the last row wears a shirt that reads *SMASH THE CIS-TEM*. There are more queer couples than straight, it appears, worshipping as if the service were the cross-stitch class Georgia attends every other Tuesday at the Danforth laundromat. She can't help but smile, overwhelmed, confused, comfortable for the first time since coming back to Port Peter. She finds a free space at the edge of a pew on the left side of the chapel.

Felicity is fully vested for Ordinary Time in a chasuble as green as summer grass, adorned with embroidered white flowers. One of her two servers—a younger person with a buzz cut—hands her a black biretta hat and takes their place on a bench near the high altar. Felicity places the biretta on her head and walks slowly but confidently up to the lectern, facing the congregation. She smiles.

Please be seated, she says. A few announcements before we begin. First, please keep Wren in your prayers as he prepares for top surgery next week. Any prepared meals for him can be dropped off here on Saturday any time before noon, and we'll make sure he gets them.

Next, Lila's book club starts in September. There are copies of James H. Cone's *The Cross and the Lynching Tree* in the sacristy if anyone needs a copy before the meetings begin.

Felicity shuffles a stack of paper in front of her. She clears her throat.

And when he had given thanks, he broke it, and said, This is my body, which is for you. Do this in remembrance of me, Felicity recites. In the name of the Father, and of the Son, and of the Holy Ghost.

Amen, the congregation responds.

I've struggled a lot with the phrasing of this passage for many years, Felicity says. Our Lord offers us Himself in His entirety—His precious body and blood—and we are to receive it in *remembrance*. But if you are anything like me, fully human, fully lacking, fully failing each day to reach full sanctification, you know that the act of remembrance is not an inherently positive thing. Nostalgia is remembrance. Grudges are remembrance. Grief is remembrance.

I speak about my late son Isaiah a lot, she says. Because we honour people when we talk about them in all their truth. When they have passed on from this world, telling their truth is a way of keeping them with us.

And the truth isn't all good or all bad. It is a lot of things. It is love and care and moments that you wish you could go back to. It is hate and fear and moments that you will never forgive the person for. It is the things we forget about, the everyday truths, the little ones, the hot chocolate and the cream-coloured sweaters and the times they were in the same house as you but not in the same room and you didn't feel happy or sad—you just felt near another person, and now you don't. All these things together, and the things we will never say out loud—all of them are the truth. And the truth can help us remember.

A moment of silence. The congregation waits.

But those truths are only for us, here, on earth, she continues. They will not bring my son back. And the absence of those truths will not upset him in Heaven. Each of us has the opportunity to decide if we want to speak those truths aloud when someone has left us. We get to decide who we share them with. Our partners. Or our kids. Or God. But sometimes, it is no one at all. Sometimes, we honour our dead in silent ways, through action. Working in ministry. Reading poetry. Drinking hot chocolate.

God is in us, always, Felicity says firmly. We are made in His image. Our very nature is one that is drawn to Him. And He gave us the power to remember. It's such an incredible power. It raises things from the dead. It can change who we are and the world we live in. But it isn't our only power. We aren't beholden to it.

Felicity's eyes scan the pews, then stop when she sees Georgia. Their gazes lock.

We are worth more than what we remember, she says.

NOVEMBER 2008

Kind does not own black funeral clothes. The Birds do not see the point of making garments that mimic the darkness. On the day of Isaiah Bloom's wake, Kind buys fabric dye from the art-supply shop on the strip and boils it over the stove, dipping a white linen dress in the pot with a pair of tongs. Rings of darkened spots on her slender fingers and a crown of silver hair pinned up and away from her face, bits of blond from past lives left on her ends.

The wake is held in the St. Paul's parish hall across the street from the church. St. Paul's only uses the building for coffee after Sunday service and for vacation Bible school one week a year in July. The vicar makes extra money by renting the space out. It is used for Lions Club meetings and quilting competitions and pickup basketball and high school MuchMusic dances and flu-vaccine clinics and landscaping conventions. There are thick wooden beams across the ceiling, perfect for hanging banners or streamers. Cream-coloured walls, and a shiny maple floor covered in black shoe scuffs.

White fabric tablecloths are draped over grey fold-out tables, lined against the wall closest to the parish hall front door. Each table has two white pillar candles and a purple ceramic vase of white roses. There are more tables on the opposite wall. Take-Twelve boxes of hot coffee that pour out at the flick of a switch, and stacks of disposable coffee cups. Wicker baskets of creamers and sugar packets and black plastic stir sticks. Hot water, and mismatched parish mugs, and individual camomile tea bags. A store-bought party plate of cubed cantaloupe and honeydew melon bordering a cup of plain yogourt and toothpicks for dipping. Cubed cheddar cheese and slices of salami. Soggy cucumber and tuna fish sandwiches, cut into triangles. Spam and Flakes of Ham mixed with mayo and rolled in tortillas, cut into pinwheels. Stacks of napkins meant for a child's baptism, each printed with the words *WELCOME HOME*.

A redwood mahogany casket sits on a platform near the emergency exit. It is surrounded by white roses. Atop the casket is a framed photograph of Isaiah Bloom. Kind had only met her grandson once: at the Happening at the Park, hours before he drowned. He is much younger in the photograph—ten or eleven at the most, with chestnut eyes and curls.

The room is crowded, but it is obvious that Kind does not belong. There is an ease with which the people walk from table to table and make small talk. They carry envelopes with condolence cards and white gift bags stuffed with tissue paper. They all seem to know one another. Kind has never felt comfortable in town, away from the other Birds. Even the farm feels different, somehow, from this. Maybe it is the tourists, who come and go and don't know that she isn't a local because they don't know what to look for. Here, people are gathered in groups of friends and families, and Kind is standing alone. She was never very good at acting like one of them—like a person. She was never very good at pretending.

But there is one man on his own as well, lingering near the back door. He nurses a mug of tea, and the steam of it fogs his wire-framed glasses. His face is shaven, his greying hair freshly dyed a stark, youthful black like his suit jacket.

Kind pours herself a tea and stands beside him. Minutes go by in silence before she speaks.

Do you remember me, James?

I forgot your name, for a while, he says. Couldn't recall it. For fifteen years. I woke up on the morning of my fifty-eighth birthday, and the memory of your face was like a haze, not quite right, not quite real, and I knew that your name was an adjective, and I shuffled through some—brave, fair, fierce—but I couldn't find it.

When did you remember?

Just now. When I heard your voice.

He pauses.

I thought she would be safer with me, he says finally. Like I could keep her from getting hurt.

Neither of us could've done that.

Are you here to bring her back with you?

I came to see you.

A moment of quiet sits between them.

I've thought a lot about what I would do if I saw you again, Kind continues. Fantasies like finding you shouting from a sinking ship, unable to save yourself. Watching you drown.

Do those fantasies make you feel better?

No, Kind says. But they are so real now that they feel like memories of real things that have happened. And I have a certain nostalgia towards them.

I understand.

It's exhausting to hate someone that much, though, she continues. Hating you made my pockets heavy. It's like, I didn't know who I was before you ruined me, so I became a time capsule instead of a person. As if remembering you was my whole purpose.

Aren't we all time capsules, Kind?

It's not all we are. I hope.

James's gaze shifts towards the casket across the room.

If I forget Isaiah, he disappears.

He's already disappeared, James, Kind says. You don't need his permission to forget him.

AUGUST 2019

Felicity Bloom wakes to the sound of her dead son's voice.

She must have been dreaming about him again, she thinks at first, her face wet with fresh tears. She leaves Georgia sleeping in bed beside her and makes herself a cup of hot frothed milk with lavender in the kitchen. But as she's sipping, she hears it again.

Mom?

The little feathers on her arms stick up.

Isaiah?

The next time she hears his voice, it is quieter, delayed, like an echo. Felicity walks to the entryway of the vicarage. Waits.

Mom?

The voice is somewhere outside, she's sure of it. She slips on one of Isaiah's knitted cardigans, hanging on a hook by the front door, and a pair of black boots.

The moon is high above the pines as Felicity walks the wooded trail, following Isaiah's voice in the distance. She lights her way with her phone flashlight. Her footsteps on the dry dirt are the beat to a symphony of forest sounds. The chirp of crickets. The rustle of branches. The flaps and shrill squeals of bats dipping low to the ground and soaring back up high like fighter jets.

Mom?

The forest trail loops from the cliffside drop with the laundry basket halfway around a small section of Lake Ligeia. The end of the trail opens onto a grassy plain overlooking the lake from the right side instead of the left. When Felicity emerges from the woods, moonlight allows her to see the white basket on the other side of the drop, separated by a U-shaped cliff above the green water. The start and end points of the trail mirror each other perfectly.

Her grandfather's lighthouse sits abandoned at the far end of the open plain, close to the cliff's edge. The front door is unlocked when she arrives.

Isaiah?

Mom?

The main room of the lighthouse is a perfect circle. Some parts of the wall are exposed red and grey brick. Others are 1960s-style worn wood panelling, cracked in places where the brick is revealed underneath. A thick steel support pillar stretches from the concrete ceiling to the stone floor and goes through a round kitchen table that has been sawn apart and nailed back together to fit around the pillar.

The room has remained unchanged since Felicity saw it last. Three wooden spindle-backed chairs surround the table, each with a green-and-yellow linen seat cushion with frilled edges.

Exposed piping climbs up the walls and over the windowpanes, leading into the kitchen. Tattered rope nets sag above a checkered orange-and-yellow loveseat, covered in circular mustard-coloured throw pillows. Side table. Record player. A glass coffee table that has turned opaque and dust brown, holding a single crinkled magazine: *Outdoor Life*, August 1982.

Mom?

Two rusted pokers hang on either side of an open brick fireplace. Felicity wipes a film of dust off one of the picture frames on the mantle. A water-damaged photo of her grandfather standing beside her father, James, with a bundle of blankets in his arms. The bundle is a baby, no bigger than an adult forearm.

The same wood panelling covers the walls in the kitchen. A long rectangular table with a green linen tablecloth and matching frilled tablecloth skirt. There are two woven carpets with tasselled edges in front of the rounded sink, with another frilled linen skirt covering the cupboard below. A matching fridge sits to the left of the sink, a little shorter than Felicity, white with rounded edges and a metal handle like that of a a car door. A china cabinet filled with tincture bottles and dried herbs instead of dishes. An electric stove and a rusted metal kettle for boiling water.

Mom?

Down the hall, a room with two single beds and a baby bassinet. Orange-and-green floral bedsheets. A vase of dried roses and a robin-shaped clock atop a green dresser. Shells and rocks and pieces of beach glass. A wicker laundry basket. A lantern. Rubber boots. Oars and a bundle of rope mounted up on the wall. The closet is filled with moth-eaten wool sweaters and corduroy slacks.

Felicity follows Isaiah's voice to her grandfather's bedroom, halfway up the spiral staircase. The walls are thickly bricked with curved windows. It is dark and dusty, and Felicity walks into a mess of cobwebs on her way in. Another single bed—another metal frame. She calls out Isaiah's name.

Her phone flashlight illuminates what she thinks is a large fishing trap high on the farthest wall from the door. When she gets closer, it becomes clear that it is a massive skeleton mounted up on the wall: a human skeleton, with wing bones instead of arms.

Isaiah? Are you here?

And she hears something, but it isn't Isaiah's voice. It is a low rhythm all around her. Movement from the lighthouse walls. Like a pulse.

DECEMBER 1986

Kind finds the Georgia squirming in the cliffside lookout laundry basket in the early hours of Christmas morning, when the sky is still dark and the air is still frigid cold.

She had watched the girl's young mother emerge from the wooded trail, her newborn swaddled in a white table-cloth. The baby kept screaming as the mother left. This was normal—Kind usually arrived when the newborns were belting their own kind of song. The best way to calm them was always to sing back. Humans could not resist the sweet calm of Bird song.

But when Kind lifts the baby girl out of the basket and begins to sing to her, the girl continues screaming and squirming.

Kind tries a different song. Slower, with a whispery tone. The baby wails and wails. And Kind wonders if, perhaps, this child can sense that Kind is not a real mother. That when her own baby girl was born, she felt terrified, and her newborn seemed alien. That when her daughter was stolen from her, the immense grief could not completely over-power her relief that her body could be her own once again.

I'm sorry, Kind says to the baby.

The girl stops crying, and her dark blue eyes rise to meet Kind's. Kind furrows her brow.

You like when I talk to you? But you don't like when I sing?

It takes Kind a moment of looking at the child to realize what is wrong. She holds her in silence, until the baby begins to shriek again. Then, Kind starts to sing again. The baby does not look at Kind until she stops and speaks.

You can't hear Bird song, Kind says.

It is a first for Kind: a baby who cannot hear her singing. And it is a problem. When the babies are taken to live with the Birds, they need a way to be called if they get lost. Bird song is sleeping medicine. It is a cure to sickness. It is a thread that leads back home in the labyrinth of the world. To bring this baby back with her would be to keep her isolated from those around her. It would be cruel.

Kind places the girl back in the laundry basket.

Please, God, Kind whispers, don't let her remember this.

Over the course of her marriage, Felicity Bloom learned how to see only the good in her now ex-husband. She saw some things, and blocked out others.

She noticed the way her husband looked at Isaiah when he recited a piece of scripture perfectly, with pride and love. She noticed the comfort and counsel he gave members of the congregation who showed up on the vicarage front steps pleading for money or food or forgiveness. Arlo gave them his own blanket off their bed. Cooked for them and lent them his favourite theology books. Paid their way when Felicity knew that there was barely enough money to get her family through the remainder of the week. To strangers, he gave and gave until there was nothing left to keep for himself. To his family, he loved and loved until there was nothing left of them to love.

He swept the hardwood floors and scrubbed food crust off the kitchen countertops and cooked bread in the bread maker just so Felicity could smell the luxurious yeasty warmth without having to make it herself. He hosted dinners for the church food bank volunteers and helped Felicity choose the organ music for each service and still somehow managed to fulfill his duties as a full-time Anglican priest, hardly paid a living stipend for his time.

She noticed the things about him that nobody else on earth could ever possibly notice. The corners of his mouth raised in a slight smile when he got a new coin for his collection. The little gasps of delight that escaped his lips when she trailed kisses down the back of his neck. How he prayed when he thought that no one was watching. Head bowed. Hands clasped. Tears spilling down his face. Begging God to make him a better man. Is noticing the good in someone the same thing as love? Can it be, if it needs to be?

But she also noticed the way her son's bones seemed to lock in place when his father was nearby. With Arlo, Isaiah could not let himself relax.

The mourning dove had convinced Felicity that no matter how harsh Arlo was with his son, his harshness only lasted a moment.

But the bird in Felicity Bloom's head is dead, now. It died when her son died.

At Isaiah's funeral, the flapping—it ceased. An absence of reassurance or advice. Just a sickening silence. The kind that swallows thoughts before they can fully form.

And the smell of rot. She could not rid her nostrils of the reek. It was so strong that she could taste it. Every time she spoke, she held back a gag, certain that her words might lead to vomit.

When Felicity forgot details of her past, the bird remembered. She would watch Isaiah walk up to the pulpit to read an epistle during mass, suddenly so much taller than she ever realized, and she would ask the bird, Do you remember? Do you remember when Isaiah was born?

He was a tiny thing, the bird told her. A hatchling. He did not cry. He was taken straight to the NICU. Hooked up to wires and given fluids through tubes. You recovered in a hospital bed and drank cups of apple juice. A nurse checked your stitches for infection and helped with the adult diapers you had to wear until you were healed.

The nurses did not give Isaiah good odds. He will not last the night, they said. You should prepare yourself. Your husband sobbed in the hospital waiting room, but you were not convinced. He'll live, you said, not a hint of doubt in your voice.

The Grande Arabella grows as Felicity and Georgia approach it in their water taxi. It is a towering ship with massive wooden masts and ripped white sails. Georgia sits across from her, wearing one of Felicity's black dresses. Felicity only owns long-sleeved dresses now. They flatten her array of red feathers, and with a sweater or jacket added on top, her condition is invisible.

We don't have to go, Georgia told her after mass, tickets in hand. I don't even have to go. But you *really* don't. Arlo will be there. It might be—you know.

Do you want to go? Felicity asked frankly.

I'm worried about Kit, Georgia said. I'd really like to talk to her on her own. And I'm leaving town in a couple of days.

I would like to go, Felicity said. I like jazz.

What if you run into Arlo?

I'm sure I can handle it, Georgia. It's a big restaurant.

Felicity accepts the ticket precisely because Arlo will be at the Grande Arabella. Expensive food. Rich crowd. Felicity dressed to the nines, clergy collar proudly on display. She will walk right up to him when she sees him, she decides. She will take him by the hand and kiss him on the cheek like they are old friends. How have you been? she will say, even though she will already know how he has been. Broke. Running a sham exorcism business on the boardwalk. A drunk with a girlfriend one third his age and a baby on the way, according to Georgia. And he will know all these things as he looks back to Felicity and remembers how he left her with nothing, with no one, grieving, no bank account, no driver's licence, no credit, no support. And he will see her now, a priest of the church he was supposed to lead. A better priest, helping make a better church. Beautiful. Thriving. Strong. Alive, without him. Alive, despite him. And she will not need to say anything else. She will be the bigger person. The better person. And this moment will be the final piece in her healing.

The dining room of the Grande Arabella has red velvet walls with dark trim. Twenty or so round tables fill the space between an old oak bar at the back of the room and a low stage up front. Kit is in the middle of her set, dazzling in a glittery red slip dress with a centre cut down to her belly button. Her hair is up in Marilyn Monroe–style pin curls. She slides her hands up and down the mic stand in perfect time to the accompanying drummer, saxophonist, and trumpeter behind her.

The women are handed slips of paper with the chef's menu selections for the evening. Beef tartar. Duck confit. Cornish hen with grated truffle.

Felicity scans the room. Her eyes search every table. No Arlo.

Georgia sips her wine with glee.

She's going on break in a couple songs, I think. I'll pull her aside then.

Felicity nods, still looking around.

Flick, Georgia says. I don't think he's here. You're fine.

Right, Felicity says.

Then, it dawns on her.

Order the hen for me, she says, lightly touching Georgia's arm. I just need some air.

She is up before Georgia can question her, weaving through tables, excusing herself, until she is at the side doors to the boat's deck: the only place smoking is allowed on board.

The air is humid out on the lake. It is dusk, and the mosquitoes are out in full force. Felicity isn't surprised that her ex-husband is the only one outside on the deck, his immediate needs outweighing the painful consequences of his decisions. Always.

He has traded the fake clergy collar for a plain black button-up, now unbuttoned to his collarbones. He leans with his shoulders over the deck railing. He throws half-smoked cigarettes into the lake, one after another. Felicity walks up to the railing, her heels clacking along the deck.

Reverend, Arlo says, taking out another cigarette.

Arlo, Felicity says.

He burps. Coughs smoke. Hits his chest until he is breathing properly again.

Are you *on duty*, as it were? he asks.

He takes a step towards Felicity, swaying, and Felicity grabs him by the arm to keep him from bumping into the railing.

You're drunk, Felicity says. You should be inside. I'll take you.

You took *vows*, Arlo slurs. To the priesthood. When you're on duty, you *have to* take my confession. No matter how *drunk*. No matter how much you *despise* me.

He stumbles again, but this time, falls right down onto the deck. Felicity kneels in front of him.

You want an absolution? Here?

Arlo looks up at her. He looks so, so tired. Like he hasn't slept in years.

He nods.

And this, Felicity decides, is how she will be the bigger person. She will absolve him, and then she will never have to see him again.

She moves her hand to make the sign of the cross. Arlo does the same, but moves right to left instead of left to right. Felicity ignores this.

Bless me, *Reverend*, for I have sinned.

How long has it been since your last confession? Felicity asks.

Eleven years.

And what sin do you have to confess?

Arlo looks back over the deck, out towards the lake water. Felicity turns her head, unsure what he's looking at.

I wasn't trying to drown him, Arlo whispers.

And for the first time in eleven years, Felicity can hear flapping behind her eyes.

Pardon?

Isaiah, Arlo says. He said—and Georgia—I don't know why I got so angry. We were on the beach and I think I just wanted to... I was...in pain. And I wanted him to be in pain, too.

The Bird in Felicity's head is singing, now. So loud that Felicity has to strain to hear her ex-husband's words.

I wasn't trying to drown him, Arlo repeats quietly. I wish I was gone, instead of him, but I'm not.

Suddenly, Arlo reaches out for both of Felicity's wrists and grips them tight. His face is an inch from hers.

It's my fault, Flick, he says, his breath scattered. And you shouldn't have to forgive me. But—but I need you to. I need you to forgive me.

He leans his head forward, his forehead pressed against Felicity's. She lets him.

Please, he says. Forgive me.

I forgive you, Felicity says.

The words fall out of her mouth, and it is both her mouth and not, both Felicity and not, both mourning dove and not. There is no precise moment in which Felicity Bloom unbecomes. There is simply a before—the pride of surviving without Arlo Bloom, the smugness with which she wished to help him simply to watch him fall apart—and an after. The after is a thing made of anger and hunger. It is not a priest, but a Bird. It is not Felicity, but something new. Something with no name.

I forgive you, she repeats, and she takes Arlo's face in her hands and kisses him.

It is more of a bite than a kiss. It draws blood.

Georgia finds Kit in the bathroom dabbing mascara from her cheeks with a wet paper towel. She sniffles until Georgia walks in, smiling through tears.

Hey, she says. You came.

You alright?

She nods, but her face contorts.

I—I don't know what I'm doing, Kit stammers. I feel like I'm drowning.

She pauses.

Do you ever regret leaving? she asks Georgia. Or do you think—do you think it saved you? To get out of this place?

I don't know, Georgia lies.

A distant scream. Wet and guttural and dripping with fear.

Later, Georgia will wonder why she did not identify the scream as Arlo's when she first heard it. She will wonder why she did not leave the bathroom right then to follow the sound of the scream to the boat deck. To the sight she will only be told about later: the pool of blood and pile of clothes and bones and flesh that once was Arlo Bloom. A woman in a white clergy collar, red pouring from the edges of her gaping mouth. A woman who is no longer a woman at all, but a Bird. Her call answered. Need met. Belly full. Feathers dripping blood and grief. A Bird who looks the waiter in the eye as she climbs the railing of the boat deck. Who smiles before she jumps into the darkness of Lake Ligeia.

And the water gladly accepts her. The water remembers.

ACKNOWLEDGMENTS

Writing *Bird Suit* has been a five-year odyssey, filled with folks who were integral to the journey.

Thank you to Jenny Berkel, Síle Englert, Misha Bower, Maggie Riggs, and Jonathan Hermina for your eyes on the early drafts of this book.

Thank you to Cassie Mannes Murray and Zoe-Aline Howard, who continue to guide my eyes back towards the humanity within my work, and the humanity within the publishing industry, especially when that humanity is most difficult to find.

Thank you to Camille Intson, who is everywhere in this book. We met when we were both young Georgias, and we both learned that we are not invincible. I am so grateful that we are not invincible.

Thank you to the Canada Council for the Arts, the Ontario Arts Council, and the Toronto Arts Council for their financial support of this project.

Thank you to my family at Invisible Publishing, including but not limited to Norm Nehmetallah, Kim Griffiths, Jules Wilson, and Megan Fildes, who breathe life into every book they touch.

Thank you to my editor, Annick MacAskill. She takes my mess of twigs and leaves and shows me the fully formed nest.

Thank you to my family in faith: The Rev'd Dr. Gary Thorne, The Rev'd Dr. Walter Hannam, Sarah, Drew, Katherine, The Rev'd Martha Riddell, Jared, Thomas, Veronica, The Rev'd Louis Harris, Tash, Matthew, Brooke, Elise, Phillip, and the rest of St. Bart's Regent Park. I thank God every day that you are in my life.

Thank you to those who supported me while I wrote a strange book about peaches and birds and grief: Sloan, Mom, Jake, Dad, Charlotte, Katherine, Rob, Parker, Meg.

Thank you to my husband, Christian, who teaches me over and over again what it means to love, and to be loved, and to live a life of love.

Finally, thank you to Stephen, Jimmy, and other Birds left unnamed. You are worth more than what you remember.

SYDNEY HEGELE (they/them) is the author of *The Pump* (Invisible Publishing 2021), winner of the 2022 ReLit Literary Award for Short Fiction and a finalist for the 2022 Trillium Book Award. Their essays on life with Dissociative Identity Disorder have appeared in *Catapult* and *Electric Literature*, and have been featured by *Lithub*, The Poetry Foundation, and *Psychology Today*. Their essay collection *Bad Kids* is forthcoming with Invisible Publishing in Fall 2025. They live with their husband and French Bulldog on Treaty 13 Land (Toronto, Canada).

Invisible Publishing produces fine Canadian literature for those who enjoy such things. As an independent, not-for-profit publisher, we work to build communities that sustain and encourage engaging, literary, and current writing.

Invisible Publishing has been in operation for over fifteen years. We released our first fiction titles in the spring of 2007, and our catalogue has come to include works of graphic fiction and nonfiction, pop culture biographies, experimental poetry, and prose.

We are committed to publishing writers with diverse perspectives. In acknowledging historical and systemic barriers, and the limits of our existing catalogue, we emphatically encourage writers from LGBTQ2SIA+ communities, Indigenous writers, and writers of colour to submit their work.

Invisible Publishing is also home to the Bibliophonic series of music books and the Throwback series of CanLit reissues.

If you'd like to know more, please get in touch: info@invisiblepublishing.com